An African Vacation

AN INTERRACIAL ROMANCE

ASPEN BERRY

Contents

1. A Ghanaian Plan 1
2. White Sands 13
3. Party Time 31
4. Aburi 49
5. An Incident 65
6. Two Transactions 81
7. Bushes 101
8. Steepled Hands 106
9. Pinnacle 122
10. A Double Case Of Epididymal Hypertension 132
11. Euphoria 142
12. Anguish 151
13. One Month Later 156
    Epilogue: Three Years Later 162

From the Author 195
Also by Aspen Berry 197

An African Vacation

After four best friends graduate from the University of Oxford, it's time to head away on a well-deserved African vacation.

For Rupert, the plan is simple; propose to Milly, his long-term girlfriend, and live happily ever after. For Montgomery, however, he'd love nothing more than to finally seduce Belle, champion rower, Miss August in the university calendar and the girl of his dreams, and what better opportunity than amidst the sun, sand and where the only male competition happens to be impoverished and, well, dark-skinned.

However, both their plans are cast into disarray when the girls soon begin taking an interest in some of the more local "attractions."

CHAPTER 1
A Ghanaian Plan

MONTGOMERY

"*L*adies and gentlemen, we'll be landing shortly, please take your seats," comes the kind of gravelly voice through the intercom that I wouldn't even trust to deliver my food, never mind land this fucking plane. I've been on edge ever since taking off from Heathrow but now I'm positively shitting bricks as we begin our descent and whatever awaits us down below hurtles alarmingly close.

Rupert raises his eyebrows. "Hey, Monty, get a load of the view."

I'm hesitant but lean across him anyway, almost to where his girlfriend, Milly, is still sleeping, looking ever the angel in her little bobble hat that was required attire back home on a freezing cold November morning but which now seems rather surplus to requirements, and I dare glance out across all the dilapidated shanty houses with scrap metal roofs. Something shines back and I'm getting the awful impression it's an open sewer snaking a passage between all the ramshackle huts where little black dots, children probably, are rolling around at play. At least, that's how I'm imagining things down there.

"God dammit, what a way to live," I mutter, still

squinting down at the traffic and congestion and smog and terrible heat that's almost certainly about to trigger a perpetual asthma attack, and I don't even have asthma. Tell me again, why did I agree to this? Oh, yeah, the obvious feminine reason sitting six rows back across the aisle. Could have gone to Tenerife instead, but no, we're modern sophisticated graduates of Oxford University, don't you know, which apparently means we're supposed to help out the world's charity cases just so that we can rub it into everybody else about how sophisticated we are. Dig an irrigation ditch here, milk a cow there, take the obligatory photo holding a bunch of starving African kids for social media before fucking off back home to our parents' mansion and a life of easy work. Well, with a bit of luck she - that is the reason I'm putting myself through this - will start looking at me a little differently when I'm providing clean drinking water for an entire village of people who are apparently incapable of doing it for themselves. I straighten and say to my best friend, "fuck it! At least we're booked in at a resort." That was the one thing I'd insisted on. My hands are bred for dealing in fine art, not wielding a bloody shovel, so damn right we're getting driven to the White Sands Beach Resort at the conclusion of every day's hard graft. Rest, relaxation, and with a bit of luck that other thing, finally. I've waited long enough for her to notice me and if this doesn't work then I can't think what will, short of becoming a Hollywood movie star, and I think it's safe to say that's not about to happen. "Fucking shit hole," I exclaim.

Rupert chews on his lip, still glancing outside. "Be good to visit the city at some point, though." That city happens to be Accra, the capital of a country that goes by the name Ghana - I know, I know, don't get me started - though I detect the hesitancy in his tone.

"You don't sound so sure?" I shuffle uncomfortably. Pretty soon we'll be landing and I'll almost certainly be pressured into trying out the local cuisine, whatever the fuck that even entails.

He makes a nervous exhalation. "It's not as if I'm ever likely to be back here…"

"Noooo…" I say sarcastically.

"But it's Camilla," he jerks his finally trimmed bearded jaw toward the athletic redhead still sleeping, and who happens to be the reigning Oxford University women's double scull champion, well, one of the two, "if we spend the whole trip lounging back at the resort, she'll never let me live it down."

I squint funny at him. "We're digging fucking stink ditches, or have you forgotten? Surely that's enough of the local culture for anyone?"

He waves it away. "You know what I mean."

My nails dig into the armrest. "So, she's really so keen to see us all kidnapped, huh? Can't you put your bloody foot down just this once?"

He shakes his head. "She wants to try some of the street food and…"

"Street food? We can pay a local gofer to go fetch us some grilled rats, Accra-fresh, and bring them back to us at the beach."

"It's not just the food, it's the architecture…"

"Architecture?" I interrupt. "I had no idea the Ghanaians, or whatever the fuck the locals are called, were known for their bloody architecture. I thought they were only known for…" I glance up and can't think of anything, so I let the subject fly.

Rupert shakes his head. "Culture…"

"Culture?" This last one prompts an obnoxious bark to escape me. "Can you even name a single famous person, piece of literature, movie or anything else that's ever come out from this entire bloody country throughout all of time?"

His eyes flick up as he goes into thought. "Ok, point taken, but there's the music…" he shakes his head in the sort of way that shows his irritation, "it might not be great but Milly will love it anyway." He peers across to the bombshell he's somehow ended up being allowed to plough, and in an instant his face softens. "I'd do absolutely anything for her, so making a trip to hear a band, or whatever, is a small sacrifice to endure."

This is a conversation I regret not having before leaving but it's far too late to do anything about it now, least of all back out of this trip entirely. "So let me get this straight … your girlfriend wants us to risk our lives venturing out into the hellscape just so we can listen to some man with a bone through his nose banging on a bloody drum?"

"Bone?" He subconsciously self-hugs. "Oh, God, when you put it like that…" I'm really detecting the nerves in his voice now but it's about time somebody other than myself was realistic about just what in the bloody hell we've stupidly got ourselves involved with here. Four white tourists walking around alone in the middle of deepest, darkest Africa; two of whom happen to have ridiculously rich parents, the other two of which happen to be more beautiful than anything this country's ever seen. Just say it to yourself. I mean, what could possibly go wrong? "Fuck, Monty," he grabs my arm suddenly, "we'll be safe, won't we?"

"I can't make any promises." I decide not to tell him about the documentary I watched before heading out, about witchdoctors and albino poachers and famine and AIDS and mosquitoes and malaria and flies buzzing around baby's eyeballs, and all the rest. It never harms to do one's research. Granted, it was from some other part of Africa, but it's all the same, right?

"Fuck! It's just that…" he checks again on his girlfriend then leans closer to me before pulling something out from his pocket. It's a small black box.

My eyes widen. "Mate?"

"Shhhhhh…" he glances back again at Milly then returns to me, "I didn't want to keep it from you but at some point I'm planning on proposing." He opens the box to reveal what has to be one of the largest rocks in Africa. "So, you see, this trip *has* to go absolutely perfect which, unfortunately, means that if Milly wants to see Accra, then Milly gets to see Accra, and I don't care whether her reasons might be to stare at buildings, listen to a bone-man banging on a drum or to eat rats, that's what we're doing."

A blast of air escapes me. "Well, she's hardly likely to say *no* to a ring *that* big! Fuck! Mate, how much did you pay for it?" I use my hand to shield the thing from the line of sight of the large black female flight attendant who keeps hovering around. Why take any risks when doubtless she'd do anything to get her fat fingers on such a precious stone. More money than she's ever likely to see in ten lifetimes.

He quickly closes the lid and stashes it away again. "Quarter million."

"A quarter of a fucking million!" I say too loud.

"Shit, will you keep it down!"

"Sorry … was just a surprise, is all … yeah, make sure you keep that in your sky rocket at all times, you never know what these people are capable of." I exhale and can't believe I'm about to say this. "Look, obviously, I'd rather not put ourselves through anything dangerous, but if you need this to go perfectly and she's likely to cause a stink about remaining safe back at the resort then, I don't know, perhaps we could hire some private security, or something," I pat him on the knee, "right, Money?"

Money's an old nickname I use for Rupert on account of his family's wealth. Let me tell you that there's rich and then there's de Beaumont rich, which is what happens when you've owned half the county of Shropshire dating all the way back to William the Conqueror. Rupert's family is the very definition of old money. "Right," he agrees, which makes me feel easier, though who will protect us from the security?

Milly stirs and a wave of pleasant peachy perfume sails its way athwart Money to assail my own nostrils. "We close, babe?" Comes her delicate, tired voice as she peels back the hem of her cute little bobble hat to reveal those sparkling green eyes that were at least partially responsible for Rupert's falling so recklessly in love, and pretty much the rest of her music course to boot, from what I witnessed. It was only at graduation the other month that at least three fellow Oxfordians had publicly wept whilst having to say their goodbyes, so I understood completely the situation Rupert was in. Men become obsessed with women like this so best tie her the fuck down before some other twat with a fat cock beats you to it.

"It's worse than that, Monty," he'd confided during our final night out together around the bars of Oxford.

"What do you mean?"

He waved it away. "Sorry, it's nothing."

I placed a hand on his shoulder. "Hey, Money, I'm your best friend, you can tell me anything."

He'd required several more shots before he could finally bring himself to tell me what was on his mind, by which point a bottle of scotch costing £5,000, a Dalmore, thirty years matured, was all but completely vanquished. He dragged a hand across his head and subconsciously glanced over his shoulder to make sure Milly hadn't entered the bar with the girls from the rowing club. "She's been accepted by the London Festival Opera."

I shrugged.

He sighed. "That means that in just a few months she'll be travelling the world with a troupe of talented, fit and athletic dancers, musicians, singers, and let's not forget the rich businessman who owns it." His fist clenched of its own accord. "The bastard made her dance for him."

I blinked. This businessman might be rich but I highly doubted his wealth could touch Rupert's dad's fortune, though I understood my friend's concerns and didn't need to contradict him on that score, because travelling the world as part of an all-singing, all-dancing troupe of talented performers hardly lends itself to fidelity. "What are you going to do?"

He wrung his hands nervously together. "I don't know, you're usually good at this sort of thing, I was rather hoping there'd be something you could suggest."

I downed another shot and allowed a moment of silence to pass so that my next words would hold more gravity. I slammed the glass down and stated profoundly, "get her pregnant!"

He turned away bearing teeth because clearly my suggestion was all nonsense. "I'm being serious here, Monty."

I pulled him back. "And so am I." I made soothing hand gestures. "Think about it for just a minute. It's kind of hard being a touring singing-dancer person when you're weighed down by a baby, no? In fact, if motherhood won't put an end to her dreams altogether then I can't think of anything else that will."

He'd rolled his eyes. "You don't have to say it like that, Monty."

"Yes, I do, because you need to get real about the situation you're facing here, and if you can't get over the idea of having to end her dreams, for her own good, then instead you'll have to get used to the very different idea of losing her to some muscular dancer with biceps, abdominals and thighs the size of your bloody waist."

His jaw had clenched at the appalling picture I'd painted, but at least he was starting to listen, albeit grudgingly.

"Look," I'd persisted, "you can't tell me you're not completely fucking besotted with the girl, you ain't the only one, believe me, so the only question that remains is how far you're willing to go to keep her. Do you really believe you'll ever get another one like Milly, even with your family's money? Because I'm not so sure." And that was the truth of the matter. She'd been Miss October in the Oxford University fresher's calendar, though I wouldn't tell Rupert I still possessed my copy from that year and revisited that immaculate image from time to time with a jar of Vaseline and a box of tissues.

He'd nodded grudging acceptance. "But do you really think getting her pregnant will put an end to this silly travelling opera idea of hers?"

I squeezed his shoulder. "It's the only thing that's guaranteed to work, that is assuming you can get her to keep it."

He waved that fear away. "Milly hates abortion, she's always been outspoken about that."

I steepled my hands. "I love it when a plan comes together."

It took many more shots, not to mention running through endless ideas and scenarios in search of an alternative for him to finally realize he really didn't have any other options. "Maybe I could go with her?"

"Oh, yeah? And how's that going to look with you tagging along wherever she goes? Cramp her style much?" I'd shaken my head. "Besides, aren't you forgetting something? You're starting work for your dad soon." Rupert de Beaumont Senior was a venture capitalist and my friend would be learning the ropes with a view to eventually taking over the family empire. The job kind of entailed having to be in London.

He'd hung his head. "Oh, but maybe she'll remain faithful, don't you think?"

"Now you're bargaining. Look, even in the unlikely event she does remain *faithful*," I invested the word with air quotes, "even for a short while, it will only be a matter of time before she succumbs to temptation, dumps you, and starts spreading her legs without any of the guilt and shame. Either way, you're going to lose her. She's in the prime of her fucking life, for crying out loud."

Rupert was gazing beyond me now, his little brown beard twisting up as he wrinkled his chin in contemplation. "You're right."

"Hey, I'm not happy about it, but I know you expect only the truth from your best mate." After a short silence, I followed with, "so now we need to figure out how we're going to replace her birth control with Tic Tacs."

He'd shaken his head. "That's just it, Monty, the pill makes her ill so she doesn't take anything."

My head tipped back as I let out an obnoxious bark. "I love it when a plan comes together." In case you haven't noticed it by now, I'm a huge fan of the A-Team. "Great, so now all you need to do is stealth the girl."

He'd squinted. "St… what?"

"Stealth." I'd slapped my forehead. "Just remove your rubber halfway through the act and then Bob's your uncle."

He'd made a sad face, which was almost enough to make me think he didn't possess the balls to go through with such a necessary plan. "I really don't like the sound of this. It's dishonest."

I nodded. "Yeah, it is, it's dishonest, and the alternative is that you'll lose Camilla to some muscular dancer who can bend her into positions your sweet and innocent little mind is completely unable to even fathom." I'd waved away his growing discomfort. "Oooooor, you could just fuck her in a dark room, wait until she's not paying attention, slip off your sheath and then finally get to know how it feels to go raw inside of your woman."

His face.

After more back and forth, he'd reluctantly steeled himself to the task and thanked me for the much needed moral support, which was when he'd made to leave.

I was keen to drag him back down into his seat.

He'd raised an eyebrow. "Yes?"

"And now it's your turn to do something for me."

His head jerked back. "Something for you? What do you want?"

I'd pretended to be paying attention to a fingernail. I definitely had fingers meant for dealing in fine art. "You know what I want."

After a moment, he'd said, "you mean … Arabella?"

I'd nodded. "Precisely. Arabella."

Rupert squinted. "What about her?" He was definitely playing dumb now. These last five years I'd made no secret about how much I liked Milly's partner in the double scull, Miss August. Talk about wanting to sail your boat into port. Those two had been the cause of many a vicious fight between the toffs and boffins of Oxford, let me tell you.

"Look, you and Milly are going to get married and have a dozen kids but soon as graduation's over, Belle's heading straight back up to Scotland and then that will be that." Just talking about it was enough to make the awful feeling of hopeless despair start churning in my stomach. I hated the thought of never seeing her again, along with that arse she'd sculpted over many years rowing in that little boat of hers. The first two years of our Fine Arts course I'd been too nervous to even talk to her but soon as Money began dating her best friend then it kind of brought us into each other's sphere. It was both wonderful and torturous because I still got the impression she merely tolerated my presence, even if there were moments I thought she might have been tempted by my wit and charm, but all that would change and become a sure thing just as soon as she found out how great I truly was. Besides, the whole arrangement was just too perfect for it not to happen. Me and Rupert are best friends same as Milly and Belle. Some things are just meant to be!

"What am I supposed to do about her?" Rupert hit back.

"Easy!" Being an ideas man, I had the answer all ready. "We should all go on a big trip somewhere." This was logical, after all, it seemed like most of Oxford's graduates were heading off around the world on excursions of all kinds, as it was simply the done thing to let your hair down after anywhere between three and five years of hard study. It would be an easy sell.

"A trip?" He'd started rubbing his chin. "That would be good for us also. Where to; Paris, New York, Berlin?"

"I was thinking more along the lines of somewhere hot." Somewhere preferably with a beach that served cocktails where I could attempt to seduce Belle." Even thinking about such a thing, of finding out if she possessed a little blonde strip to match the hair on her pretty head, made my body tremble with anticipation. "I'll pick up some Tenerife brochures and you can plant them around in Milly's vicinity. With a bit of luck she'll convince herself it's her own idea and from then on it shouldn't be too difficult bringing your best friends along for the ride, right?" And after that, hooking up with Arabella, finally, would be logical and sensible. Because I was a great guy and we'd make a wonderful foursome.

And that, dear reader, is how we ended up taking a volunteering abroad programme in none other than Africa - Fuck my life! - because Rupert truly is incapable of putting his foot down when the women decide they really want to do something. The plan is for Rupert to propose to Milly (probably in the misguided hopes he then won't need to stealth her) and I fully intend on finally getting together with the girl I've been infatuated with ever since our first day at The University of Oxford.

Now, I twist around and spot Belle several rows back, and immediately feel the twitch from beneath my khakis. I was upset when she hadn't been able to sit with us on the flight, all because the idiot who designed this plane only thought to put three seats on every row, but I'll make up for that after arriving at our resort.

"What the fuck?" I mouth the words as I catch her still talking to that enormous African in the giant bowl of fruit moo-moo who'd clocked her as early as the departure lounge. I mean, there's being polite and then there's humouring it all a little bit too much. Belle and I make eye contact and I'm quick to turn back towards the front.

"Cabin crew, please take your seats for landing."

We land in Africa!

CHAPTER 2
White Sands

My bag's last to come off the carousel and I'm quick to seize it, remove all four locks, and start rifling through for missing items.

"Are … are you seriously doing what I think you're doing?" Arabella asks in her sultry Scottish accent with her gorgeously sculpted arms standing all akimbo.

I lift up my spare khakis, socks and underwear. "My iPad's in here."

"So?" Seriously, the way she stands looking all peeved with her breasts pushing out her purple Oxford rowing jersey in a way I can see the hard nipples beneath almost makes me pass out from the heat, and we've only been landed five minutes.

I ignore the four, now five, dark-skinned passengers whose path I'm blocking whilst I make sure everything's present. "So? It's worth a lot of money."

She rolls her eyes and tugs Milly away. I find my iPad and rest easy, reapply the locks and heft the bag before catching up, though not without cramming a fist in my mouth from the impossible sight of Belle's buttocks stretching the tight denim of her light blue jeans.

I'm telling you, but rower's physiques! When you're competitive on the sculls, like Milly and Belle, you have to arrive early in the morning four times every week to put in the hours on the river. Multiply that by many thousands of strokes propelling heavy oars through viscous sludgy water, utilizing legs, arms, your entire body over a five-year period and the end result is that you end up with a body something like these two women. Fuck! It kind of makes me regret joining the poker club, fun times, sure, but even I must admit that I have a body like a well-fed ham.

"Fucking Christ," I growl under my breath, my eyes still burning a hole through her jeans, "but if I'm not busting a nut inside of that thing soon then I think I'm going to explode." I've foregone wanking off these last two weeks in anticipation of this trip and what I'm hoping to do to Belle, though now that my balls are heavier and more tender than at any point in my lifetime, I can't say for sure I've done the right thing. No, this is definitely about to test my endurance like never before, and there's nothing quite like a sackful of prime seed to cloud one's judgement. I only pray it will all be worth my discipline and sacrifice when I'm taking her cunt out for a test drive … prior to then putting on some serious fucking mileage.

It starts immediately upon stepping outside onto the dense, overcrowded and fume-filled concourse, our white flesh and therefore obvious superior wealth and station like red to a bull, and we're descended upon from all sides by no fewer than five Africans.

"Beautiful!"

"Yes, yes, you're very pretty."

"Tell me your name."

Who am I kidding, it's the women they have an immediate infatuation with, and I find it astonishing the way Rupert and I might well have been completely invisible, a total fucking irrelevance, when for all they know we *both* could be in relationships with them. I mean, I expected harassment to a certain extent, but nothing could have prepared me for this. One of the creatures, wearing the jersey of some European football club or other, comes especially close to Belle and places his hands together as if in prayer.

"Let me show you Accra! Let me show you Accra!"

All I can do is wave my arms frantically around in the air (I might also have screeched a bit) in the hopes someone, anyone, a cop or whatever, might come to our rescue. The two rogues closest to Belle seem particularly keen, her long blonde hair tied back into a tight bun an obvious fascination to such creatures.

"Awe, thanks, that's so sweet," Belle touches a hand to her heart and blows out air as she glances nonchalantly about the chaos as though she was at the Royal Ascot, "say, I don't suppose you might be able to, possibly, find us a taxi, could you…"

Three of them are already rushing off, pushing through the crowd of arrivals, shoving people aside and gesticulating urgently from close range to different drivers. It's the gangly black wearing a knock-off Versace shirt with the underarm stains who's first to beckon us over, and as we jostle our way across the concourse it's hard to forget there's at least another two still hovering around us.

We collapse inside the taxi, slam shut the doors, and I call out an order to be taken with haste to the White Sands Beach Resort. We start moving as Milly and Belle blow kisses to our accosters come apparent saviours.

"Please, don't encourage them," I hiss but neither of the girls listen. I glance across at Rupert, who's been quiet throughout the entire ordeal, and find that his skin has turned an even whiter shade of pale than usual.

I breathe and once we start moving I get my first good look of Ghana - yes, really, we're here. I'm surprised by the fact the motorways are actually drivable and aren't covered in debris and overturned vehicles. For whatever reason, I've spent the last few days with the movie I Am Legend running through my head but the place is nothing like that. Every time we stop at lights our car gets surrounded by people selling boxes of tissues, bars of soap and other sundries, but London's much like this these days, though there are street vendors selling all types of food, which isn't quite so common where we come from. I do, however, gawk at the spectacle of a woman carrying a large basket on her head. Neither is the heat quite so suppressive as I'd anticipated. Sure, it's hot, but nothing I've not experienced on a beautiful summer's day in the south of England.

I'm sat in the back hemmed against the door with the driver's seat in front pushed so far back that after the long flight I have a right to fear deep vein thrombosis.

Belle's up front talking animatedly with the driver as though he were some old friend she's not seen in years. She has a certain way with people that's both enchanting and aggravating, the latter because I don't like her talking to other people at all. "Everybody looks so happy," she declares with sparkling eyes, "and what's that place over there?" The driver responds but does so in the kind of coarse voice I have no hope of comprehending.

After half an hour we pull into the resort. Belle insists on paying and hands over a large tip in the kind of discreet, elegant way that's all part of her charm. The driver grins bright white teeth, "thank you, thank you," and drives away.

The place is magnificent. A long beach with sun loungers and umbrellas, clean sand and palm trees. There are other people here on holiday but not so many that it's crowded. I can't wait to check in so that I can kick back with a cocktail and start working on Bella.

I now nudge up to her and give her hip a little bump with my own. "When you have a spare moment, there's something I'd like to discuss with you."

"Oh?" Her delectably trimmed blonde eyebrows pull closer together. "Sounds ominous."

"No, no, no, it's a good thing I've got for you. Promise."

She gives me a funny look and speeds up her walk to come level with Camilla out in front, which is when I realize my hands are clutching my nuts. I yank them out from my khakis and clench them into angry fists.

"Easy, buddy," it's Rupert who's dragging both his and his girlfriend's cases through the sand, "it'll happen, don't worry about it."

"That's easy for you to say, at least you get to see some fucking action." I sound more tetchy with him than intended, though it's hard not to feel a little frustrated, all things considered, and my gaze passes across Milly's arse cheeks in turn, which are every bit as hard beneath her jeans as Belle's. I'm dreading that moment I first see our female companions in bikinis because I'm not sure how I'm going to cope.

He ignores me, which is probably for the best right now, and I'm left the remainder of the walk towards reception to reflect upon my lack of sexual experience. Contrary to what you might believe, dear reader, I'm not, in fact, a virgin, but have had sex a total of three times in my life. Once with an escort in Istanbul when I turned eighteen and twice with the girl who works at Happy Cakes in Oxford, which was about as much of her as I could stomach. This was just after Rupert and Milly had started dating, bringing Belle and myself for the first time into each other's proximity, and I'd hoped that seeing another girl would make the true object of my desires view me as an enticing challenge. As it turned out, it felt like I was cheating on Belle, even though I wasn't, which is something I can't quite explain. To make matters worse, there's something about being seen with a two hundred and fifty-pound land-whale that lowers your sexual market value yet further, so my plan backfired terribly.

Arriving at reception, we're handed cool towel wipes for

our hands and faces, which is beyond refreshing after the flight and heat and dust, and then we sit in wicker couches with a glass of champagne each whilst we wait for the reception staff to photocopy our passports. After that we're taken out to a buggy so that we can be driven to our chalet.

"Awe, how beautiful!" It's Milly who points up to a parrot sitting just a few feet above our heads as we roll under it. "And look." She now points to a monkey running across the lawn. "How adorable."

I glance across at Rupert, whose face is going all gooey-eyed and soft. Fool's as besotted as I am.

One advantage of having Money as your best mate is that we get to stay in the most expensive chalet on the resort. We come to a stop outside the largest patio with its own pool and unrestricted view of the Gulf of Guinea that washes up on the beach a mere spitting distance away.

We jump off the vehicle and I hand my bag to the driver/porter to carry it for me. I turn to Rupert and ask, "what's this place costing again?"

"Eight hundred pounds a night," he says as though it's absolutely nothing, which to his family it isn't so I feel no shame in taking advantage, besides, he owes me for the whole stealthing idea, which is why back at Heathrow I'd pulled him aside to remind him of the fact, and that at some point on the trip I'm likely to call in the favour.

"And we're booked in for the full two months?" I double-check.

"All going to plan, yes."

That's potentially two whole months copulating with Belle, and come the end I fully intend on my balls being drained beyond all salvation and my little soldier being red raw and sore from overuse. I can't imagine ever getting bored of ploughing Arabella's arse. The very thought causes another twitch down below but this time I manage to resist cupping my balls, after all, there are ladies present.

The little man unlocks the door and shows us inside. It's nice. Spacious. All the mod cons. And the view of the ocean's quite incredible. Rupert's already going for the champagne chilling in the freezer so I take the opportunity to tell the porter to drop the bags because I can take them from here.

Remembering how cool Belle had looked a few moments before, I slide a hand into my back pocket and pull out a wad of notes, all smooth and James Bond-like, whilst checking from the corner of my eye that she's watching. She isn't, so I cough loud into a closed fist until she does.

"Here you are, my good man," the note says 200 Cedis and has an image of six people you wouldn't trust to clean your toilet, never mind run a central bank, but regardless, I hand it over and watch, a little confused at how thrilled he is to receive it. I clap the dark-skinned man hard on the shoulder. "Maybe buy a little something for the wife." How much did I just fucking give him?

"Thank you, sir! Thank you, sir!"

Belle's already heading away so I follow after her into one of the bedrooms.

"Oh, snap!" I say as I dump my bag onto the mattress at the same time she does.

She nods once and remains silent just long enough for it to be noticeable. "Very funny."

"Yup." I wrap a hand around the strap but don't make to move immediately. It's a nice king-size. Fucking wasted on one person if you ask me. I'm glancing around the rest of the room now. En-suite. Widescreen. Minibar. Ceiling fan. Spectacular view. I'd have been truly happy sharing such a room with Belle. A small whimper escapes me and I have an overwhelming urge to grab my balls and squeeze. The fucking insane shit this woman causes my brain.

"Are you alright?" She still has her ample blonde hair tied back revealing her flawless, pale neck and when she moves back into the arms akimbo position she sends a wave of lavender splashing over my face.

"So you're really taking this room, huh?" *Two full weeks worth weighing them down.*

She winks playfully. "Looks like it." She turns around as though the subject's closed and my gaze instinctively roams down her back, the way her waist nestles tightly between broad, slightly muscular shoulders and expansive hips built for bearing my children, buttocks I have absolutely no idea how she manages to squeeze inside the denim of her jeans, and muscular thighs and calves. There's not a damned thing I don't want to do to her over and over again. She begins bringing shit out from her bag, perfume, feminine deodorant bottle, a red fucking bikini, but stops suddenly to stare at me. It's a few seconds before I'm even aware of it. "Montgomery?"

I snap to. Why the fuck does she call me the full protracted version of my name, it's terribly impersonal. "Sorry, I'll … find another room." I don't tell her that I fully intend on returning at some point in the not too distant future.

That other room turns out to be the living room and the other bed happens to be the wicker couch. Sort of makes it obvious that I'm the lowest down on this group's totem pole.

"It won't be for long," Rupert reassures me as he hands over a glass of champagne.

"I fucking hope not," I take a swig, "I feel like I'm going insane and we've only been here ten minutes."

He gives a sympathetic smile. "Just play it cool, mate."

I nod. "Yes, that's, um, great advice, cheers." Easy for him to say. He probably bust his nut inside of Milly only this morning. Maybe I should just retire to the bathroom for a quick wank, get it out of my system so I can think straight, I can't imagine it'd take any longer than a couple of minutes in this state, and I take the first couple of steps but stop, deciding against it. *Just think how good it will finally feel to make your deposit inside of her snatch.* Fuck, maybe she'll let me do it unprotected?

The door to the master bedroom opens and out steps Milly wearing a yellow bikini and a gym bag slung over a shoulder. I make a double take, disregarding Rupert standing beside me completely, as my left knee starts to quiver from the sight. Damn fine woman, one of the best rowers in England that she is. Miss October aside, I realize I've pretty much only ever seen Camilla wearing her rowing club jersey, and while that might be cute there are limits to what it can do for her figure. *This* I wasn't prepared for, large perky boobs with just a few freckles typical to redheads and abdominals just faintly visible beneath a slim waist set within an hourglass figure. The long red locks left to roam halfway down her back is the clincher and I have to resist the urge to readjust my shorts.

That is until the other door opens and out steps the love of my life wearing only the red bikini I'd spotted earlier. I feel a *whooosh* aimed straight at my heart as a bead of sweat rolls down my back. My cock's throbbing and my knees very nearly give way entirely. I've seen her body, that heavenly image of Miss August forever scars my soul but *this* I was not prepared for at all. She was a fresher when that photo was taken five years ago, an eighteen-year-old girl, beautiful, sure, but she still had some maturing to do, physically. Now, as I gaze at her, there can be no doubting Belle's all woman.

"We all ready for the beach?" She says in her Scottish accent that alone is enough to turn me weak. She hitches her little sports bag and adjusts the strap of her bikini bra that's struggling to contain her gifts. Damn, but there's something about the colour red on a blonde.

"Yeah, we're all ready." I think it's Milly who responds and then I feel a nudge in my side.

"Monty," it's Rupert who's whispering, "you're making a strange whimpering sound."

"Huh?"

"I said play it cool, man."

"Oh," I shake it away but I'm still gawping at Belle and her absolutely flawless skin, no blemishes, scars, not even a bloody freckle. Surely, God would not be so cruel as to put me with such a girl if it wasn't going to lead somewhere.

She struts past in the sort of way that has me questioning whether she knows what she does to me, and that she might even be enjoying it, and a minute later we're all kicking up sand as we make our way along the beach towards the sun loungers.

The waves roll gently up to our feet before retreating, and the coolness washing over my flesh offers some gentle relief against the heat. Ahead, people are kicking footballs, jogging in the surf, lazing back enjoying cold drinks whilst the kids build sandcastles, and there's even a game of volleyball underway, what looks like a mixed group of Europeans taking on some locals.

What's truly eye-opening, however, is the sheer quantity of European sex tourists, all women, in their late fifties and beyond, sixties even, strolling across the sand hand-in-hand with young African men as they spend money that was undoubtedly as good as stolen through divorce settlements. At least they're all old and washed up, I tell myself, and will not be bringing little half mud babies into the world, not that such a fact would lessen any embarrassment for the children left back home.

My attention is seized by one such woman, probably because she's far younger than most of the others, possibly her late thirties, maybe forty, and although she's well-fed and big-breasted, she's most definitely not hard on the eye. She reclines back in a chair with a glass of white wine, her long brown hair unkempt and messy as it tumbles down towards the sand. She yawns for an especially long time and then lazily brushes the shoulder of the enormously muscular grinning brute massaging her feet. I wonder about her story, if she too is recently divorced or whether she's only just come to realize she's missed out on the marriage and family boat entirely and is now angrily lashing out at the world.

Of course, we men do this sort of thing all the time, travelling mostly to Asia to sample something exotic, but it's different when we do it, we're men and it's to be expected. For women to engage in this sort of behaviour, however, leaves a particularly nasty taste in the mouth. We grow up being told the fairer sex is different, that they aren't quite so sex-craved, and, yet, here they are, and their presence can only leave me questioning much of what I've been led to believe. For the Africans involved; either the lure of a potential European visa must be all-encompassing, or the very sight of white flesh, no matter how shrivelled and ghastly, must turn their knees weak.

Wanting only to spare Belle from the appalling spectacle, I now side up to her. "That thing I was wanting to discuss…"

"Oh, yeah?" She touches up her sunglasses in a way that shows the small swell of her feminine biceps.

"Yeah, I was thinking, but you're moving back up to Scotland soon, right?"

"Correction, I've already moved back home."

I feel something drop in the pit of my stomach, her answer convincing me that I have to go for broke this trip. "Awe, shucks, that's too bad. Is there much work going in the world of art dealing up there?"

She shrugs and I can already tell she's given the subject much thought. "Some. Maybe in Edinburgh. Glasgow, perhaps. But not much up in Inverness." She makes a sad face. "After this trip I'll probably have to start handing out applications for Starbucks." She sighs. "I wouldn't be the first grad having to do that so there's no shame, it's just .. you know, the obvious thing."

"Right, it's not what you spent five years studying for, is it?" Sensing that we're actually making a fucking connection here, I dare touch her bare shoulder and feel the most wonderful tingle shoot up my fingertips. "Well, here's the thing … it's just that Horace, Archibald, Barnaby and myself are opening our own dealership close to the Embankment." Prime London real estate if ever it exists and if this doesn't impress the girl then I can't think of anything else that will. I bat at a mosquito. "Anyway, I was thinking, we could always use a pretty face front-of-house, you know, to charm prospective buyers," she's turning into me now and I feel the hope start brimming in my veins, "and since we already know you, well…"

"Oh, my gosh?" She clasps her hands beneath her chin and makes a cute little jumping motion with her body, in fact, for a brief second I almost think she's about to give me a hug. She doesn't though. "That sounds wonderful, oh, but Barnaby and I don't get along, not after I turned down his advances at last year's sports ball."

What? That really happened? I'll tear his fucking throat out. Shit, but she turned him down, right? That has to count for something. I'm not sure how enraged I ought to feel about this news, and the truth is it's thrown me a little off my path, though somehow I manage to bring myself back to the important task at hand.

I again dare touch her shoulder and find myself encouraged by the fact she lets me do it. "Now, now, Belle, don't you worry about him, he knows the score and won't be causing any problems for you, that's a promise."

"Oh, but I wouldn't wish to be the cause of any friction between the four of you."

I wave away her silly fears. "As I said, you leave Barnaby to me." Wow, this is going really well. Of course, I won't tell her the venture's being almost completely funded by my parents, as well as Barnaby's, because that doesn't sound anywhere near as impressive, so I'm happy to let her assume I'm the man carrying the burden of risk who can therefore expect the greater share of the reward going forward, but this is going great nonetheless.

"Wow!" She removes her sunglasses to look at me and I almost dare hope there's something beyond appreciation in her eyes, might I even dare say it, desire. One thing I've learned from reading gigabytes of dating advice online is that women love a man who grabs the world by the balls and right now, I'm certainly demonstrating that quality. Thanks, dad, for the money. Barnaby's too. She slowly shakes her head in disbelief. "You know, I think that's really ballsy starting up on your own like that, and straight out of Oxford too."

"Hmm, yes, I know."

"Can I think about it?"

I absorb her praise like Super Mario does a mushroom. "Of course, take your time. No pressure." I close my eyes and take a deep beautiful breath of ocean breeze. With a bit of luck she'll be riding me cowgirl style within the first week.

We reach the sun loungers and order cocktails, though being of the ginger persuasion, I'm careful to avoid those hazardous rays as much as possible, grabbing an extra umbrella for double the shade and shoving the point as deep into the sand as possible. My three companions are taking different precautions, slavering their flesh with copious quantities of sun lotion and my mojito very nearly goes down the wrong pipe when I turn around to find Milly rubbing the stuff across Belle's back and shoulders.

I have to turn onto my side to conceal the stiffy threatening to explode inside of my shorts but that preoccupation is soon overwhelmed by a loud cheer coming from the volleyball game where hugs, handshakes and high-fives are now being exchanged between the two groups of players. A second later there's a large black guy wearing only a pair of baggy yellow shorts peeling away from his team and who is now jogging through the sand in our direction.

"Oh, hello, who's this?" It's Belle's voice that prompts me

to turn back towards her and when I do she's prodding down her sunglasses to take a peek from above the rim in that way people do when something's caught their attention. The light plods of feet on sand draw nearer but I'm only prompted to turn back towards it when a large clump of sand is kicked all over me.

"What the fuck!" I screech.

"Sorry, man, I am so sorry." A large black hand clutches around my entire wrist and squeezes, which I'm taking to be this creature's way of apologizing.

"You stupid fucking…" I spit out sand and have to blink it out from my eyes, which are on fucking fire, my mojito's ruined too, and I'm just about to further chastise the dopey cretin and demand he buys me another when he lets go of me, leaving behind a thick coating of rancid sweat, and positions himself in front of the other three.

Through the stinging blur, he makes a small, friendly bowing motion, not over the top, just enough to show he means well, despite all but blinding me. "Welcome to White Sands." He comes up to his full, considerable height and motions outwards to encompass the resort, and even with arms outstretched his biceps bunch from beneath his soot-black flesh.

"*Hello there,*' Belle says a little too enthusiastically, but I realize she's only being friendly because that's the kind of girl she is, despite the fact the newcomer has just come pretty damned close to committing an assault upon one of her group, or maybe it's because the word 'Lifeguard' is emblazoned in red up the side of his shorts, I can just make out through the fire that is now my eyesight, and that this imbecile apparently works here.

He brings his arms back down into his sides which, in turn, now make his pectorals bulge impressively. "All newcomers must play volleyball." It sounded a bit too much like a command for my liking, his voice like the early rumblings of Krakatoa, and has that very distinct accent common to all sub-Saharan Africans that I'm already beginning to find irritating.

"Oh, yeah?" I snarl whilst using the ice from my soiled drink in attempts to cleanse my eyes.

"It is customary," the large, unwelcome interloper insists.

"Oh, well," Belle grins a little too much towards Milly, "if it's customary then, I guess, we have no choice." I have to remind myself that Belle's friendly nature is partly why I'm totally in love with the girl, though there can be no denying there are times I find it incredibly jarring.

"That is correct, you have no choice" the lifeguard, if that's truly even his job description given I've not yet seen him take one single glance towards the ocean or the children presently swimming around in it, now gestures with a black hand to the two girls, "you two especially." He says this last bit deadpan, though there can be no misinterpreting it as anything but overt flirting. Surely, I can't be the only one who noticed, although Rupert merely continues rubbing lotion over his shins as though he was on the beach at Brighton (gay central).

The girls look at each other and answer together, "ok." They stand and, naturally, I'm paying close attention to how much our unwelcome intruder ogles them, and which girl in particular. "Let me just get my..." Belle bends down to retrieve her bag from under her lounger, bringing her arse together with its full considerable curvature to within two feet of the African's crotch.

He doesn't move and the way his lips peel back to reveal the brightest white teeth you've ever seen is infuriating.

Belle straightens, throws her towel over a shoulder and gives her water bottle a shake. "Let's go." She and Milly start walking down to the net where there are two other black men standing watching us. The Europeans who were playing before are now trudging off defeated through the surf.

"You play?" The lifeguard asks Rupert in a way that sounds more like an order.

"Me?" My friend asks as though it's the most ridiculous question in the world, which it is, and like me, you need only take one look at Money to know he's hardly the sporty type. "No, no, you go ahead and I'll support you all from back here."

The large black man turns to me, still grinning. "You." He's already stooping down and again his clammy meat hook wraps around my wrist. Talk about presumptuous.

"No chance," I point to myself, the belly overhanging my waistband, "does it look like I want to play your stupid game?"

"Come play," he tugs again and although he barely seems to be trying I can feel my body being hefted from the seat, "play with us."

I'm definitely getting the impression he feels that after kicking a shit load of sand in my face that we've already shared a certain bond, a small amount of camaraderie, and that therefore he can attempt to manhandle me without complaint. "No, leave me be, I'll pay for another drink and try to make it through this one, alright?"

"No, no, you must play."

"Fuuuuck!" This last is because I've been hauled up by the arm, he squats down, places me in a fireman's carry and when he rises back to a full stand I'm spread across his shoulders as though I'm light as a rag doll. He sets off and I'm jolting around senselessly, my arms dangling uselessly on either side of his moisture-laden torso I'm trying so hard not to touch, and I'm wanting so much to object but find my voice is squashed out by his shoulder digging into my stomach, forcing the air out of me. He picks up speed and jogs towards the approaching net, his every bounce punching my belly, all the while Milly and Belle are standing there with opened mouths.

I'm finally placed down on the opposing side and can feel my face burning with rage, embarrassment, no small amount of emasculation and probably the early onset of sunburn. "I told you, I…"

"Come on, Monty…" it's Belle who calls across from the other side of the net, using the shortened version of my name, "we're on holiday, let's have some fun."

"Fun," I growl to myself as my two apparent teammates pat me on the back and say their names, though I'm in far too much of a foul mood to even care, never mind comprehend what they actually said.

Meanwhile, on the other side, my tormentor's introducing himself to the girls. "I am Kojo," is what I think I hear from across the divide, though that can't be right, surely. What a ridiculous bloody name. He maintains a hold on Milly's hand for longer than what seems necessary, though when he comes around to Belle it's bordering on being indecent, even if she's far too polite to make any objection.

My fists clench but then I realize something. "Hey," I call across, "isn't it supposed to be whites versus nig… um…blacks?"

"Hey, it is ok, you play with us." It's Miscellaneous African Teammate #1 who tugs me to where he wants me to stand.

"Kojo play with your women," sniggers Miscellaneous African Teammate #2 whilst placing a certain emphasis on the word 'play' that has me wanting to ask what the fuck was meant by it.

Instead, I ignore them, and when I glance back across the net the motherfucker's still holding hands with Belle. "Come on then!" I shout, suddenly determined to win this bloody match and maybe claw back some lost dignity, and if, somehow, I can make this Kojo idiot look stupid in the meantime then I'll gladly take that too.

Kojo throws up the ball in a way that makes his deltoids

burst through his flesh and then gently bops it over the net. It comes slow and I dash forwards hoping to spike the fucker straight at his bloody chops but I misjudge the required amount of forward momentum and instead topple flat on my face.

I hear laughter from as far back as the cocktail bar, spit out sand and grab the ball that lands with a soft plop beside my arse.

"It's our serve," Milly says, as though I'm supposed to know the rules.

"Right," I throw it back to Kojo, who then serves to one of my teammates. The ball returns to Milly, who spikes it hard and accurate in my direction. I move to block the thing but can't get there fast enough and instead it smashes straight into my nose. There's a moment's disorientation as my eyes blur out and when they regain focus there are splodges of red tainting the sand around my feet. Still glancing down, I now see the dribble of blood coating my chest. "Milly!"

She's shaking her head. "Sorry, hun, I did hit that one a bit hard, didn't I."

I pinch at my nose to quell the bleeding and stump off back towards the sun loungers, though not without first sparing a word for the oaf responsible for all of this. "Are you happy now? I said I didn't want to play!"

There's only silence as I'm stomping away.

CHAPTER 3

Party Time

MONTGOMERY

I've spent the last hour back at the chalet lying supine on the wicker couch, my head propped on a cushion while I try to recover from the loss of blood. Just to stamp an exclamation mark upon my misery, my skin's starting to itch, particularly around the back and shoulders, which tells me I'm sunburned and pretty soon things are about to become real fucking uncomfortable.

Alone, staring up at the ceiling fan that brings its pleasant, relieving breeze, there's nothing much to do but ponder things with Belle.

The remarkable thing is that in all the time I've known the girl, I'm unaware of her ever having been in a single relationship. Our degree was pretty full on, to be fair, especially during the final three years, and she seemed to spend all her free time out on the river anyway, though considering the way she looks, it's all really quite incredible nonetheless. Of course, there was that close fucking call with … what was his name now … oh yeah, Bradley, who rowed for the Pembroke College Boat Club because he was studying Economics, don't you know. That was only last year, and I remember watching the pair of them together in their rowing outfits after training, a tall man with broad shoulders, arms sculpted from a few million repetitions heaving his big, heavy oar, and wavy blond hair she ran her fingers through as their lips met. I'd clutched my heart and that night had wept myself to sleep, and then a few days later the sexual assault allegations from what had been an old liaison dropped, putting an end to their courtship, mercifully, before it had even got off the ground.

Twenty-five thousand pounds!

That's what I had to pay the girl to make the allegation.

But it was worth every penny knowing that I wouldn't have to see them together, flirting outside the boathouse, kissing under the tree canopy, to be tortured over mental images of what they were doing in the bedroom.

I had to act quick on Bradley. Thankfully, these days, internet sleuthing is easy. Find him on Facebook and keep scrolling through until you discover information or photos that are potentially incriminating. Less than ten minutes it required to find out his group from Pembroke had gone to a bar not longer than six months previous. Squinting my eyes at one particular photo, I found Bradley in the background, seated with a brunette on his lap as they kissed. She was tagged. After that it didn't take long to discover the girl was a struggling student with debt up to her eyeballs, working part-time at KFC.

I guess twenty-five grand for a morning's work was an easy decision for her to make.

And the best thing was I'd been there to watch, after practice, when a police car rolled up to the river and in front of Belle, his teammates, everybody, he was taken away to be interviewed.

For four months his name was dragged through the mud and all thanks to the local media, by the end of it there was barely a blade of grass in Oxford that did not know the name Bradley Beauclair. He was kicked out the rowing club, off his economics course and, best of all, Belle ran a fucking mile.

Do I feel any guilt? One might be tempted to ask such a thing of me. And ordinarily the answer might very well be *yes*, after all, I'm not a complete monster. But after seeing him kissing Belle and knowing everything else he undoubtedly wanted to do to her, no, any and all compassion I might have had no longer existed.

And a thousand times, I would do it all over again.

Oh, don't get me wrong, looking the way Belle does, I'm under no illusions there'll be the occasional Chad in her past, I'm realistic about that, and the very thought of it makes me want to find them and ruin all their lives too.

But for now, I just hope I've made the point, dear reader, that there are no lengths I will not go, no depths I will not stoop, for Belle, to ensure that I have her.

The door opens and in steps Rupert and Milly.

I sit up, scratching my head. "Where's Belle?"

Milly bounces for her bedroom with an unsettling happy smirk plastered on her face while all Rupert can do is fidget with the strap of his bag. "We left her at the pool bar with that Kojo guy."

My head snaps back. "You did what?"

He flaps a hand as though it's nothing. "She wanted to stay for another drink."

I grab a clump of ginger hair at the back of my head and tug. "And you really think that's a wise thing to…"

"We need to talk, Monty." His face clams up in frustration. "One moment." He takes his bag to the room and returns, making sure to gently shut the door, and his girlfriend inside, as he does. "I'm sorry, yes, we left her, but she's a big girl and besides, there's something on my mind so pardon me if I'm not my usual, considerate self."

I'm still thinking about Belle potentially being left in danger to care much about Rupert and whatever his latest problem is, but he sits in the wicker and drags me down beside him.

"I needed a word in private because," he glances towards the door to ensure it's still shut five seconds after he closed it, which just goes to show how paranoid he's feeling, "there's something I didn't tell you … I mean … it's not big, but in some ways it is … urgent, I mean."

I need to run to the bar, quick, and drag her back. "Well, go on, spit it out and be quick about it."

He's wringing his hands together now and even his usual trim brown beard is looking unkempt. "It's just that … Milly … she came off her period on Wednesday … and … today's…"

"Monday, right, will you stop stammering and get on with it."

"Right, well … doesn't that mean it's possible to … to … to get her…"

"Pregnant today! Yes, it's possible, though unlikely, given that by the sounds of your incoherence she'll start ovulating tomorrow."

"But, Monty," he drags a hand back over his closely cropped brown fuzz, "can't sperm survive inside of her … her … her…"

"Her cunt for five days," I shake my head and blow out air, "yes, it can, which is why I said, yes, it's *possible* to…"

"So wouldn't it make sense to do that thing you suggested as soon as tonight." Wow, somehow he managed to get that last part out in one go. Credit to the man. And for once he actually has a point.

The realization momentarily concentrates my mind away from Belle and onto my dear friend Money. "Now I know why you're looking so agitated." I can't help but glance towards the still closed door myself. "Listen, don't let Milly see you like this, whatever you do, not least because you risk giving the game up, it's just not attractive. Get a grip of yourself, man."

"That's easy for you to say, Monty, you and Belle aren't sleeping with each other."

I stare suddenly very hard at the man.

"Sorry, I didn't mean … never mind." His hands clamp around my shoulders, causing me to wince from the onset of sunburn. "Do you really think I can do this?"

I shake him off me. "As we've already been through on a number of occasions, it's not a matter of '*can*' you do this, but more a matter of '*you absolutely fucking must*'."

"But how?"

Now I'm momentarily stumped. "How? You … you don't know how?"

"Of course, I know *how*, but not the specifics of the *how how*."

I slap my forehead, but eventually let out a sympathetic exhalation. "Ok, listen up. First of all, make sure the room's as dark as you can possibly make it, alright?" I glance outside and because it's approaching six in the evening in November, the sun's already beginning to set, which will help. "If it's still light outside for whatever reason, lighting, the moon, then you need to block that shit out. No TV!"

"Alright."

"Get her horny as fuck! Nibble on that cunt like your relationship depends on it, which of course we know it does, and only when she can't take it anymore do you rubber up."

"Rubber up?" His eyebrows pull comically closer together. "But, I thought you said…"

"That's because she has to *think* everything's normal, duuurr, so rubber up, as usual, and let her *see* you doing it. Then, good sir, assume your usual starting position…"

"Missionary."

"Of course, but don't stay there. At some point you'll have to flip her over. Her hands and knees would be your best bet, and even better if you can push her face hard down into the mattress so that she can't twist around." I pause for effect. "Now, my son, this is the moment of truth. You'll have a few seconds with which to part with your scumbag, so be single-minded about the operation, no hesitating, do you understand?"

"I think."

"And roll it off, from the root, no tugging it, otherwise she'll hear the slap of the recoil, and you don't want that because then you'll be left having to explain why you've just removed your brat catcher, and judging by the way this conversation's going, I highly doubt you possess the wits for such a heated exchange. If in doubt, play music from your iPhone, that should cover your tracks, but no TV!"

"But won't she be able to feel the difference?"

"Not if you've been ramming her hard during missionary, which is why you need to fuck that cunt insensible."

He nods uncertainly. "What do I do with the rubber once I've…?"

"Shove it up your arse, I don't know." I sigh. "You know, you might have to keep the banana burka in your mouth until such time as you can flush it."

He grimaces. "Serious?"

"Hey, I never said this would be easy." I give him a reassuring pat on the shoulder. "I'm sure it's not your usual kink but don't worry, it's your own girlfriend's snatch it's been rubbing up against."

"Erm, ok," he nods reluctantly, "anything else?"

"Getting her drunk beforehand might help, and then tomorrow you'll do it all over again." Which reminds me. I stand, remembering my preoccupation prior to this riveting conversation, and make to head immediately for the bar when suddenly Belle appears at the door, saving me a trip and restoring my peace of mind.

She enters holding a paper carrier bag in each hand,

followed by Kojo with the same, who bobs his head beneath the lintel as he takes it upon himself to strut inside of our home like it was *his* name on the agreement. What was that about my peace of mind? I get an immediate unsettling feeling about this. I glance quickly to Rupert and then back to Belle and hold out my palms questioningly.

She places the bags down on the countertop. "Kojo suggested we throw a party here tonight, you know, first night in Africa and all that."

"Oh, did he now," I fold my arms as I watch the brute placing his bags down beside the others.

"Yes, Monty, my friend," comes Kojo's deep voice that sounds not unlike two tectonic plates grinding together, "it is tradition." And then he does something so unexpected and so outrageous that I'm left completely fucking stumped by the action. He places his enormous, muscular black arm around Belle's shoulders and pulls her into him like he owns her. She's still wearing her red fucking two-piece bikini and as ever, he's only togged in his baggy, apparent, lifeguard shorts, and the image of his flesh, black as ebony against the brightest of beautiful white that is my Bella is a complete and total fucking abomination. Speaking of tradition, but if this was the good-ole days then right now this cretin would be answering to a rope.

I can't help but dwell on it for an amount of time I'm not even sure about, but when I manage to pull my gaze away for long enough to clock Rupert's reaction, I find him already staring at me, himself unsure what to say or where to even look.

Finally, it's Belle who breaks the tension that I can't for sure even say she's noticing herself. "Kojo was telling me all about his country's traditions. Oh, it's such a rich, cultured and wonderful place." She tilts her head to rest against his pectoral, which is all about where she comes up to on the man who must be half a foot over six, at least, and then steps out from his arm to begin emptying the bags. It was all done so casually that any neutral observer might think they were best buds.

Milly comes out from the other room wearing her pyjamas, yawning. "Oh, I thought we were eating in the resort restaurant tonight?"

Belle holds up two bottles of spirits and gives them a little shake. "Change of plans, hun."

"Oh, ok," Milly's eyes definitely flick across our unwelcome guest's torso, notably his very prominent abdominals, as she steps towards the countertop and takes one of the bottles for inspection, "Akpeteshie?"

"It's the national spirit of Ghana," Belle says in the sort of way that convinces me she's literally repeating what Kojo had said to her earlier, "it's distilled from palm wine." She too makes a lingering glance toward Kojo that confirms it, as well as sending a stab of pain shooting straight through to my heart.

I've had enough of this. The first night of any holiday is supposed to be the biggest, best and largest, sure, but we'd already made plans to eat at the resort restaurant. I step closer to the Ghanaian, who's since taken it upon himself to start raiding our fridge for bottled water. "Listen, um, Bobo?"

"It's Kojo," Belle answers for him with a touch of crabbiness.

"Right, well, it's just that we kinda, sorta already were about to head for…" there's a loud, obnoxious bang against the large plate-glass window that reveals our view of the ocean, only now all I can see is a gang of Africans, mostly large men waving their arms about.

Instinctively, I leap back with a shriek, but then Kojo declares, "ah, the party has arrived."

He strides towards the patio doors and slides them open and then four, five, six, eight, ten Africans are strutting inside already jiving to music blaring from one of those ghettoblasters you see in 80s movies held aloft on a small, thickset man's shoulder. I count eight men and two women, quite an imbalance, which means shit could get rough if this Akpeteshie turns out to be half as fatal as I suspect it will be.

I'm still watching them entering our accommodation, more food and beers are brought in, while all I can do is wonder about the local bylaws on trespassing. I sniff at the air and mention to the straggler, "maybe best leave the door open."

Within seconds the women are on the stoves cooking food, the men are using their teeth to pop beer bottles, the music's (what sounds like some African garage monstrosity) cranked up to the max and they're all dancing because, well, what else did you expect?

I turn to Rupert, who like me is looking strangely glassy-eyed right now. "What in the bloody hell just happened?"

"I … I have absolutely no idea."

Kojo's lining up the shot glasses and teases Belle by poising with the spout above her glass before retracting it.

"Oh, hey, no fair, come on," she bumps his thigh with her hip, "I really want to try it."

He holds the bottle aloft and declares, "we offer the first shot to the gods." I roll my eyes even as Bella's enthralled and he heads off for the opened door, both our girls trailing after him. He then tips a small measure into the grass before making a sign with his hand towards the sky. "The gods are satisfied. Now we may drink."

The girls cheer but it's cut short when I challenge, "aren't you all meant to be Christian in this country?" Indeed, the invader's even wearing a small silver cross dangling from his thick neck and that's somehow managed to lodge in the deep blocky crevice of the line separating his pectoral muscles.

He doesn't even flinch. "It is tradition."

"It's sacrilege, is what it is," I pluck at his cross and let it fall back against his chest, "I thought you Christians were only supposed to honour the *one* God?" I know I've got him, though I decide against going as far as calling him a fraud who's likely only wearing the thing to put women at ease.

"Hey, shush, you," it's Belle whose hand is on my arm and although I'm stinging from the small touch, I fight back the pain in order to enjoy it as much as I can, while feeling the inevitable twitch down below, "you'd be surprised by how much Christianity and Paganism have intertwined their customs." She has me there, so now I'm eager to change subject. To my surprise, she guides me gently away from Kojo. "Listen, Montgomery, I know you're still a bit peeved at him for…"

"I told him I didn't bloody want to play volleyball!" I snarl. "Why couldn't he have just left me be?"

"I know," she says soothingly, "and he's awfully sorry about what he did."

"Really? He told you that, did he?" I jab a thumb over my shoulder from where somehow I can feel his dark eyes watching us. "Can't say it himself?"

She shrugs her delectable bare shoulders I just want to run my tongue over. "I'm sure he will when he gets a minute alone with you." That's something to look forward to. "He likes you." She truly says. "He says you're a funny guy. Anyway, listen, I know you don't like him, you got off on the wrong foot, I get it, but…" and her eyes now slowly roam in his direction in a way that almost makes me sick, "you know, he works on the resort, so he's going to be around for the duration of our stay and, you know, I *like* having him around."

"What?" It comes out as a hiss.

"Well, he's interesting and we're here to make friends, right?" The way she said *friend*, it was like how I might say *business acquaintance*, and now I don't know what to think, if whether or not, after my initial shock, I should now be relieved, at least partially. "Just as we're friends, right?" Ok, now I have absolutely no idea what to believe, but if she thinks for one minute she's friend-zoning *me* then she has another thing coming.

I blink away my confusion. "I'm getting a beer."

The food is surprisingly good, what turns out to be meat on skewers, plantains and beans. Other than that there's the usual party food; sausage rolls, crisps and sandwiches. Outside, one of the men has also found some wood and has fired up the brick BBQ to cook some more meats.

After the first hour more people arrive, including my two so-called teammates from the before ill-fated none game of volleyball, further tipping the gender imbalance in a dangerous direction. I blank them completely. A game of limbo starts on the beach, the women (the black ones) especially are keen to demonstrate their prowess, dancing beneath the stick whilst pulling in their skirts and thrusting up their breasts. There's little doubting it's some sort of primitive mating call like how an ovulating chimpanzee thrusts her swollen arse into the male's face to signal how badly she wants it. It's dark now but there's a good moon and on the sand someone's gathered enough tree branches and other oddments to light a bonfire large enough to potentially cause concern. Again, what the fuck are the bylaws in such a place?

The beers and spirits continue. As expected, Milly and Arabella are quite the centre of attention, particularly amongst the men, and I definitely detect the occasional hostile glare coming from the African women present. It doesn't matter where it might be in the world, but black men desire our women over and above even their own, *especially* their own, and there can be no denying it drives their women crazy, as well it should, though to compare both groups of women standing so close together, it's not hard to see why. Of course, I'm biased, as I've never been one to pay much attention to black women, and as already established I'm holding an extremely bright torch for at least one of the British girls present, and have a deep fondness for the other, but the fact there's a constant throng of dark-skinned men surrounding the white girls demonstrates well the truth of the matter.

Kojo, however, for the time being at least, isn't one of them, as right now he's busy juggling with five skittles, three of which are on fire, and the crowd quickly concentrates around him for the spectacle. I spit beer into the sand and turn away towards the chalet interior, where Rupert's standing alone in the bar area pretending to be engrossed on his phone. I know what he's doing. He's doing exactly what I'd be doing if I had valuables stored just through the door beyond and there were so many uninvited people I didn't trust suddenly imposing themselves.

"I'm looking into hiring some private security," he looks up to make a small, appreciative glance, "you were definitely right about that."

"I've always trusted my instincts," I say, leaning back against the countertop whilst staring straight outside at the obvious person.

Now, Kojo's resting on one knee, his arm outstretched at a forty-five-degree angle. I can't hear the words but it's clear he's giving Belle some instructions. She slowly leans back against his hand so that he's pushing against the small of her bare back and then, slowly, he comes to a stand, lifting Belle up as he does. The crowd all cheers and claps, an incredible feat of strength and skill, Belle raised aloft into the air in a single one of Kojo's hands. He places her carefully back down onto her feet and she spins around to clasp him into a tight embrace.

"Yes," I say with a lowered voice, "I've always trusted my instincts."

"What was that?" Rupert asks.

"I said something around here fucking stinks." I whip out

my phone. "Let's take our first African selfie." We smile as I take the snap and when I check the result and zoom into the background, I'm dismayed to find Belle and Kojo are visible in the shot, *still* with their arms around each other. I stomp back outside and when I approach the man he appears to greet me with a genuine warm smile.

"Monty, my friend," he places his arm around me, the burn now even more noticeable, though I'm keen not to show pain or weakness in front of him so I resist the urge to wince, though perhaps the sweat from his arm that I can feel seeping through my shirt is another reason to discard his sticky embrace.

"Can we have a word?" I'm extremely conscious of the fact Belle's watching and that beside this big African I must look like a barely pubescent teenager. "Over there." I make a jerking indication with my head towards an unoccupied patch of beach.

"Anything for you, my English friend." His arm's still around me as we walk but he removes it when we're in a quieter place. "What can I do for you? I hope you are enjoying our hospitality?"

I won't say that it appears like *we're* the ones hosting *them*, no, and neither do I want to be this man's friend so instead I'm keen to get straight down to business. "Listen, Kojo, it appears there's almost certainly been some kind of confusion with regards to Belle."

"Belle?" In the dark it's impossible to see even the smallest detail from his face, which usually helps in being able to tell what people are thinking but not saying, an advantage that right now he definitely has on me, and now I regret walking so far from the fire. "What about her?"

I tilt my chin up. "The thing is, Kojo, I know she's an attractive girl but you appear to have made the assumption that she's single and that therefore you can…"

"She is not single?" It's not a challenge, no, if anything he sounds genuinely confused. And it's not that I would ever dream that Belle would even consider coupling with an African anyway, good God, the very idea is beyond ridiculous, but the issue is that he's cramping my style and getting in the way when I need to be putting moves on the girl myself.

"No, she is single but you misunderstand me … what I'm talking about is that you came straight up to us, looked at her, then at me, and made the assumption that we couldn't possibly be together, despite the fact we're a pair of twosomes on holiday." This detail had taken a while to click but now that it has, it bothers me immensely. That Belle and I were indeed a couple would be the logical deduction to make, even if it's not true, but either this mere lifeguard, and a work shy one at that, failed to even consider it or, if he did, cares not in the slightest.

He's silent for a moment. "I … I do not understand. She is not single? Because she told me she *is* single." If true, this information is truly abysmal. Did he ask or did she volunteer that information? Or is he intentionally trying to fuck with my mind?

My entire right arm is literally shaking and if this man was smaller and weaker, I might have been tempted to take a pop, especially if I knew I could get away with it. "Look, she's as *good* as spoken for, alright? Just so that you're aware, Rupert and Milly are in a relationship, and Bella and I are soon to be, hmmm-kay? So I'd appreciate it if…"

"Aaah, my English friend," he claps me on the shoulder and I have to bite back the agony, "you have absolutely nothing to worry about where Belle is concerned." Buuuuutttt, to his credit, he actually sounds fucking reasonable now.

"I … I don't?"

"No, Monty, my friend, I want you to trust me when I say

that I have absolutely no interest in your friend Bella. None whatsoever."

"Really?" My head jerks back in pleasant surprise. Maybe this Kojo guy isn't so bad after all.

"Yes, really, we are just friends, that is all, besides, she really is not my type." The sheer arrogance of the man, the way he makes it sound like he *could* have her if only he wanted, which I beg to differ. "And after what you have just said, I can only wish you the best of luck with capturing her heart."

A relieving blast of air escapes me. "Well, that's great, erm, does *she* know that, um, I mean, are you really sure you're not…"

"You have nothing to worry about, Monty, my friend, trust me, for I am already engaged to my childhood sweetheart." His face might be all but completely invisible but he sounds genuine enough and my instincts are telling me to believe him.

It's a beautiful feeling, that of relief, and I hold out my hand for him to shake. "Congratulations. That's great news and I'm very happy for you both, erm, when's the wedding?"

He swallows my hand in his and gives it a few pumps. "We are getting married in June, seven months from now, and you can believe me when I say that it has been a long time coming."

"June?" We won't be here for it. Shame. "And what's her name?" Just making sure.

"Her name is Ashantay and I love her very much." He doesn't even hesitate and I'm left actually believing it, truly, but then why wouldn't Kojo be engaged to some lucky African woman? A remarkably good-looking man, impressive stature, bumps, swells and crevices in all the right places and immense charisma, as much as I hate to admit it. "Monty," he again guides me with an arm around my shoulders in the direction of the chalet, "let us celebrate our new friendship over an Akpeteshie."

I wouldn't have put it quite that way (and still no apology for the volleyball fiasco, you'll notice, or for kicking sand in my mojito) but I go willingly enough, and although I might have been deliberately avoiding this noxious sounding spirit, I decide on giving it a whizz regardless, after all, one must keep up their own end for the sake of appearances, and we *had* just come to an understanding. Passing Belle, Kojo's arm still around me, I can't quite help but feel like a dog being led around by his owner, but I recognize that this feeling's all inside my head and that nobody else is thinking it.

He fills two glasses with the golden fluid, the fumes alone are enough to choke a well-fed rhino, and passes one to me.

"Um, what proof is this?"

He nods, "yes."

We clink and there's a small moment of hesitation as I wait for him to down his shot. He does and his Adam's apple bobs, a second later his chest, shoulders and abdominals involuntarily tense in a way that makes visible the veins and striations beneath the thick musculature. He blows out air and runs a hand back over his closely cropped woolly black hair. "Drink, my friend."

As everybody knows, I'm partial to the occasional dram of whisky, particular if it comes with a hefty price tag and somebody else is paying, so I bring the poison to my lips and knock it straight back. It takes less than a second to feel the fire scorching its way down my throat and oesophagus before landing in my belly where I'm sure that even now it's dissolving my stomach lining. My rapidly blearing eyes fix on the bottle, 55%, and the next thing I know I'm dashing for the refrigerator, tugging out a carton of milk and spilling half the contents down my shirt as I rush to quell the flames. I hear laughing from close by.

It's Kojo. "We will make an African of you yet, my friend."

I'm not even sure how I spend the next thirty minutes to an hour, a combination of imbibing any and all milk I can grab, dashing in and out of the bathroom and, for all I know, attempting to make out with one of the African birds (although you can be sure I'd first need several more shots before succumbing to *that*).

"Monty, are you alright?" It's Rupert's delicate voice that ricochets through my head.

"Save or craig!"

"Inscuse me?"

"Save or fucking craig!" I growl at the man. Must everything be repeated when it hurts so much to talk?

When finally I find my equilibrium, I stagger first for the support pillar in order to show my appreciation for the fine job it does in providing us with a stable structure before eventually managing to make it outside. Briefly, I consider running through the bonfire, but manage to put such thoughts out of my mind for now. No, it's time to do something even more reckless, I don't know, like finally, after five long years, telling Belle exactly how I feel about her.

There are more people around now and most of them are looking at me.

"Belle?"

More funny looks. People stepping away.

"Belle?" I reach for the nearest dark-skinned reveller and he spills beer over the lip of his bottle. "Have you seen Belle? Or Kojo?"

"Kojo!" He points in the general direction over the other side of the chalet so I head off over there.

I've not yet had chance to look around the resort, so I'm wary about wandering too far off on my own when it's dark and, let's face it, I'm more of a juicy target than most. "Belle?" I crash into some sort of upright and less than a minute later fall into what's possibly a rose bush. Hauling myself out, I pluck thorns out from my skin. "What am I even doing?"

She's probably back at the chalet with Milly drinking tea. I straighten my shirt and head for the bonfire's glow that's silhouetted around the edges of our building though, feeling suddenly very tired, I pause for a rest on an adjacent bench…

And throw up all over my shirt and khakis.

Because sitting beside me are Belle and Kojo, their arms pulling away from each other as their lips quickly part.

CHAPTER 4

Aburi

MONTGOMERY

Our driver arrives in an open-topped Humvee to transport us to the place we'll be spending the duration of our stay volunteering, a village that goes by the name Aburi. We were told it would be a fifteen-minute drive from our resort but after close to thirty, we're still rumbling along a narrow dirt track kicking up dust and occasionally getting whacked in the face by errant branches. I'm getting the impression that under delivering on big promises will turn out to be an African trait.

But what do I know anymore?

Ever since downing that lethal shot, I seem to have lost track of space, time and perception completely. For example, I keep seeing baboons out in the thick vegetation but Milly insists she read they're not found wild this close to Accra. The truth is I'm seeing flashes and probably the occasional hallucination, so I'll be damned if I trust my own eyes and ears anymore, and that includes visions of my worst nightmare come true, that of finding Belle smooching those thick black lips of Kojo's as he envelops her in his enormous muscular arms. All this is why I very nearly skipped our first day of punishment in favour of recovering back at the resort. In the end I opted to come only because I hated even more the idea of parting with Belle, even for a day, especially while there are still question marks about what awaits us in Aburi.

Finally, we arrive in the village, which is pretty much what I expected; a wide, flat expanse of dirt dotted with trees and the occasional mud house fouling the landscape. The smell of what has to be shit openly fermenting in the sun infused with distilling Akpeteshie wafts across on the barely relieving small breeze along with the mosquitoes.

Immediately upon exiting the vehicle we're crowded by a hundred kids all running, jumping, cheering and clambering for us. Unable to resist, Belle and Milly crouch down for hugs and cuddles, scooping up the occasional tot in the sort of way that immediately demonstrates their ingrained maternal instincts, while Rupert offers his hand for high-fives. I almost do likewise but then spot under a canopy of trees a boy squatting down taking a shit before wiping his arse with a small square of cloth before dunking it in a pail, wringing it out and repeating the process. I'm not sure why but I'm the only member of our group the kids aren't jostling as we make our slow and obstructed walk towards the community building in the centre of the village.

"Hi," Arabella waves to a white man straining with a wheelbarrow filled with bricks, who nods back in return, and then we pass more of our kinfolk, all men, carrying out a range of arduous physical tasks; bricklaying, plastering, digging. One man's on top of a mud hut applying thatch to the roof while another's using a foot pump to drain the contents of a cesspit into a waiting tanker.

I bat at a mosquito. "And these fools paid *them* for the honour?"

"We did too, Monty," Rupert reminds me.

"Oh, yeah," suddenly the joke's not so funny. What was it

we paid the agency? That's right, £1500 for the two-month duration. What was that about Tenerife?

We discover the whereabouts of the women volunteers at the community centre, which is also the village school, medical facility and shop. Six of them, including a couple of definite lookers, one of which could easily pass for a supermodel and whom I can't peel my eyes from, are drinking coffee in what counts as a staff room.

"Heeeey," "Welcome to Aburi," "Nice to meet you," I hear in a number of accents as everybody gets up to introduce themselves. Milly and Belle especially are given warm welcomes, such is the way of women, while Rupert and I wait for them to come around to us. It's now I notice that one of the women, a tall brunette with a French or Swiss accent that I wouldn't ordinarily look twice at, is very heavily pregnant while another, unfortunately the slightly lesser of the two attractive girls, is sporting a bulge all of her own, albeit far smaller.

"Hell of a place to come when you're expecting," I say in a quiet voice for Rupert's ears only.

"I know," he mumbles back, "think of the hepatitis."

"Syphilis, herpes, AIDS."

"What are you two conspiring about?" It's the supermodel who, mischievously, steps right up into my personal space.

I'm so taken aback that all my instincts are telling me to move back a step so that I can regain my poise. I'm only stopped owing to the tight confines of the room and Rupert being flush in the way.

"Sorry," she runs her hand down my chest by way of apology, even though from the look of her smirk I'd say she's not sorry at all.

All I can smell is rose petals and it's the most delightful scent in the world. "Oh, you know," I manage to keep my voice calm, measured and even deep, despite her physical perfection, "only our plans to unify the Ga-Adangbe and Mole-Dagbani tribes under one banner to take Accra before conquering the whole of Ghana with me as their king and deity." Seriously, but if I wasn't so besotted with somebody else there's no way in hell I'd be able to even talk to a girl like this.

She lets out the most adorable laugh and then her fists are nestling against my chest as she recovers. "Perhaps, then, I can be your queen?" Fuck! I'm in deep shit here, real deep shit. Finally, she holds out her hand. "I'm Ingrid."

I take her hand and dare linger with it. "Stockholm, by any chance?"

Her mouth plunges open, revealing the most perfect set of teeth sans even a filling. "Yes! How did you know that?"

"I was there last Christmas on a ski trip. Your accent ain't getting away from me." I'm extremely struck by her beauty, what's likely a girl of twenty-two, perhaps twenty-three with long wavy blonde hair left free to roam down her back and three very stylish braids, red, green and blue weaved in. She has a small ring through the left lobe of her nose, which is far from my usual thing, in fact she has a bit of a hippy vibe generally, but with Ingrid I can most definitely make an exception, and her blue eyes give the impression of great intelligence and an immensely good nature. In fact, I'd say she's the embodiment of every man's ideal Swedish blonde.

"Oh, that's a shame, you never called on me," our hands still connected, she pokes out her bottom lip that all I want to do is nip between my own.

"Well, I'm sure somewhere there's a volcano around here we can board down together?"

Her hands are back on my chest again as her body descends into a fit of trembling giggles. "I might have to hold you to that." She brushes hair out from her eyes. "How long are you here for?"

"Two months. How about you?" *Please don't say you're leaving tomorrow.*

"I arrived last month with Greta," she points to one of the women that owing to her blandness I'd barely even noticed, "we're here for six months." That'll do nicely.

Don't take me the wrong way, I'm realistic that if we were anywhere but the middle of the fucking jungle then ordinarily a girl like this would not give me the time of day, but here and now, where the extent of male competition consists of me and the guy sucking shit from a giant hole in the ground (any local Africans being in the *not applicable* category, for obvious reasons), it would appear that a month is all it takes for this fat, out of shape ginger to suddenly find himself somewhat acceptable, even to a supermodel. No matter what, however, I'll be more than happy simply to make a new friend as this is definitely a cool girl.

"Half nine, ladies, duty calls." One of the other women taps Ingrid on the shoulder and she looks at me apologetically.

"I guess, then, that I'll be seeing you around." She bounces once on her toes.

"Definitely." I watch her exit the room with the others as the most wonderful buzz surges through my veins.

"She was definitely flirting with you," Milly says, unable to hide her happiness, or is it surprise.

I kind of know she was but I would still enjoy hearing it from someone else. It might never happen again. "Noooo, she wasn't. What, really?"

"Durrr." She shakes her head, grinning. Stranger things have happened.

However, what happens next truly takes the cake, because as I so often do, I go to make eye contact with Belle, only this time she's already looking at me and makes quick to avert her gaze. But I saw it! I definitely saw it. Something I've not seen from her ever and, might I even dare contemplate it, but being familiar with the emotion, I might even have recognised a tad bit of jealousy?

There's a moment of silence as we wonder what we're supposed to be doing, which is when the door opens again. It's the heavily pregnant brunette with the French accent.

"Hi, Marie," Belle offers, inflecting up the name so that it sounds like a question.

She blows a loose strand of brown out from her face. "Rupert, Matty?"

"Monty." I correct her.

"Go find Jimmy out in the village. He's the guy from Ireland and he'll show you what you're doing." She smiles at our two women. "Belle, Milly ... Winston will see you now."

There's a moment's confusion as they both glance at us. "Aren't we going with the guys?" Milly asks.

Marie opens the door further, a touch of impatience flicking across her features that she quickly manages to mask. "Don't worry, you will, but Winston likes to make sure everybody's best used according to their talents."

I'm biting my tongue, fighting the urge to argue that *Winston* hasn't met Rupert or me either, but instead we both head meekly out into the mosquito infested early morning sun without saying a word.

"An Irishman can't be hard to find around here." I'm taking in the village where we'll be spending the next two months. Not much here. The mud huts are scattered around the place in and amongst the dust and trees, nearly all with piles of debris heaped against the walls, including the occasional oddment that forces me to question just how in the heck it got here; a typewriter, grandfather clock, broken tables, even a bloody car door that looks like it came from a Mini Metro. Women perch outside shacks grinding spices, kneading dough, weaving skirts. I see one elderly woman, maybe late thirties, pouring a canister of what has to be petrol into a large plastic tub.

"She's distilling Akpeteshie," Rupert says, "no wonder we found you unconscious in that loading bay."

"Right." One thing I notice, as we spot a short red-haired man in the near distance, is that there are no males, at least not of the native variety, save for the occasional very old man leaning against his home. Either they've all moved to Accra to find work or, perhaps, they've gone further afield to Europe.

"Looks like a slimmer version of you." Rupert chuckles as we approach what has to be Jimmy plunging a shovel into the ground.

"Ah, more victims." It's an obvious joke, though he says it so deadpan that it's hard to tell. We're introduced and he seems like a friendly enough guy, freckly, short ginger hair.

"So," Rupert claps his hands together, "what are we working on here then?" He sounds more enthusiastic than I feel.

Jimmy nods at his shovel. "The plan is to do away with the cesspits and build a sewer system that takes the waste away to a location at least a mile out of the village." I should have known. "As you've probably guessed, our job is to dig the trenches that'll take the shit away." He plucks up two shovels that were conveniently waiting for us and hands them over. "Nice and deep, lads, and if you find any bones then just toss them over there."

We spend the morning digging. In places the ground is like rock and so we have to jar our shoulders hacking away at it with the pick. As it turns out, Jimmy's been in Aburi almost seven months, work experience prior to becoming a priest, or so he says, and he's so keen to talk about his African experiences that I get the impression we're the first company with this task he's had.

"People come and go, obviously. There are fellers here from all over the world. Richard's from Argentina, Duncan's from Australia, we've got Germans, Spaniards, even a fucking Pole, and there's me thinking the cabbage munchers hate to travel. Kenny, you know, the guy pumping shit out from the hole over there … turns out he's from Wexford, only a short drive from me."

"Dirty convict labour," I remark without giving any further opinion, "and what about the women?" I can't help but think again about Ingrid, not to mention Belle, who I'm already missing. So far I haven't seen a single woman pitching in with the toil.

Jimmy lets out a sudden sharp exhalation that almost sounds contemptuous. "The women? Winston likes to keep the women close to him." There's definitely something in his tone that merits further discussion of the topic.

Rupert and I just happened to be thrusting our shovels into the earth at the same time, and now we come to a stop, glancing at each other. "What do you mean?" My friend asks, doubtless thinking about Camilla and how she's being occupied this morning.

Jimmy too thrusts his shovel into the ground and leans against the handle. He's wearing only a sleeveless vest revealing slender, freckly arms with some of the most appalling sunburn I've ever seen. He's now giving us a certain look that I don't quite know what to make of.

The silence prompts me to ask, "and who is this *Winston* guy anyway?" I shrug. "We didn't get chance to meet him … must be busy, I guess."

Another blast of air escapes Jimmy. "Busy? Aye, that's one way of putting it." He goes on to explain that Winston's the man appointed by the agency to oversee the project for this village and that he is, in fact, not Ghanaian at all, but from Jamaica, having returned here after tracing back his roots. "At least that's his story, which took long enough to get out of the guy, and not for lack of trying." He scratches at his arm and causes an avalanche of dead skin to flake off into the trench.

"Let me just tell you that the phrase *'laid back'* fails to do him justice, and yet at the same time it describes him perfectly." Rupert and I share another glance. "Pah!" Jimmy continues. "I'll let you make up your own minds about Winston," he invests the name with a certain something I can't quite put my finger on, though it makes me feel more than a little concerned considering he's the guy supposedly in charge around here. Two whole months.

After only a couple of hours, my future art dealing hands have already developed calluses and my back's beginning to ache like a bitch. Regardless, I pluck up the shovel and continue digging. Keen to change the subject, I ask, "so what happens when we've finished this trench?"

Jimmy jerks his head further along the existing trough. "You'll find Gabriel up there laying the pipe, and I don't mean that in the sexual sense, despite being Marie's husband, if you know what I mean." This time, his tone is definitely filled with bitterness, and now I'm beginning to wonder if this Jimmy chap is just an extremely negative man we're somehow stuck with.

Not knowing what he means, Rupert and I give each other another look. This, however, is interrupted by the very welcome sight of Ingrid striding through the village in our direction.

I can't help but immediately cease what I'm doing to stare at her long, slender, golden legs as they step over the uneven ground that, to my eyes at least, almost seems to level out of its own volition before her dainty feet. Men, women and children all stare as she passes and, at least to my ears, it almost sounds like there's an uptake in the singing coming from the exotic birds high up in the nearby trees.

Jimmy whistles. "Definitely one of nature's better creations. What I wouldn't give not to be a devout Catholic for just one night." He shakes his head and scratches again at his sunburned arm.

It occurs to me that as an atheist I'm not lumbered down by any such religious restrictions, though I'm still having trouble believing I'm in with a shot regardless. What happened before, it must have been a trick of the light, as well as my mind, I mean, last night I'd imbibed a shot of something it turns out they use petrol to distil.

She ignores Rupert and Jimmy completely, instead stepping straight up to me. "I'm just calling everyone in for lunch."

Damn, that smile. If I didn't already know it, I do now. I'm in big fucking trouble.

LUNCH IS TAKEN in a large outdoor play area behind the community building. The kids are already seated and the noise is loud and incessant, but there's a happy vibe to the place and I'm glad to be enjoying a well deserved rest. Most of the female volunteers are all together at a table on the other side of the yard and Milly waves to us through a gap between the children. To my surprise, Ingrid arrives with her plate and sits next to me.

"So what brings you out here?" I ask her, given that I'm more than curious to know everything about the girl.

Her green braid is particularly errant and tumbles down her cheek. "I had a choice between Vancouver and Aburi for work experience as part of my degree in Medicine at Stockholm," she actually says as though it's nothing, "I figured that Aburi needs me more, so here I am."

If I wasn't impressed with Ingrid before, I certainly am now. A fucking doctor, wow! Seriously, why the fuck is she even humouring me? I place my spoon down beside the bowl of cooked beans and chicken everybody's eating. "That's … that's incredible."

She flaps a hand as if to suggest it's no big deal. "Well, if I ever want to be a doctor then I *have* to be here. What really impresses me are those who give up their money and time willingly coming out here to volunteer." She smiles in a way that makes me think she's talking about *me* personally and not *we* generally.

We chat for a while as more white faces arrive for lunch and I learn that most of the volunteers are living in Aburi; in various houses, camping, or in the small dormitory right here in the community centre. Richard, the Argentine with long brown hair tied back into a man-bun, introduces himself and takes a seat at the same table along with Jimmy and Rupert. Then, finally, I get to meet Gabriel, who's a striking man and reminds me of Henry Cavill, the guy who played Superman, only with stubble and longer, unkempt hair that betrays how long he's been away from civilization. Oddly, as soon as he sits down it's as though a switch has been flicked and Jimmy's body angles away. Without a word, Richard stands and leaves.

It's now that I'm drawn to the movement of a door opening on my left and then the attractive woman with the early signs of pregnancy shuffles into the yard. Jimmy notices too, the mere sight of her prompting him to silently shake his head.

Curious, I lean closer to Ingrid and quietly remark, "people here don't get along, do they." And perhaps that, now that I'm thinking about it, might have something to do with why she's so keen to make friends with me. Cynical, I know, but it's still so hard to believe given the last girl who paid me this much attention weighed a hundred and fifteen kilograms.

"That's Cathy." Ingrid says nothing more because I'm thinking she's just too nice to want to say anything negative about anybody.

"She's a cunt," Jimmy, evidently having no such qualms, helpfully adds, "you'll soon see why. She can't help herself."

I can only watch as Cathy approaches Marie, the other pregnant woman who looks like she's about to pop at any moment, and whispers something into her ear. They then switch places at the table before the Frenchwoman plods this way and drapes her arms around Gabriel, who now I recall Jimmy saying is her husband, words are spoken in French, they share a shameless kiss that's borderline indecent so close to us, not to mention a hundred kids eating lunch, and then they're both walking, arm in arm, towards the door that Cathy just exited.

Jimmy must see my confusion because he exclaims, "looks like they've been summoned to see the boss." He throws down his spoon and stands to leave. "No wonder nothing gets done around here."

"Ok," I turn to Ingrid, "can somebody please explain to me what in the bloody hell is going on?"

She flaps a carefree hand. "Jimmy's just upset because he liked Cathy but Cathy likes Winston," she gestures in Cathy's direction, presumably referring to the small paunch she possesses, "and as you can see, Winston likes Cathy too."

"Ah." The sense of revulsion instinctively bubbles through me, as happens every time I see a black man with a white woman. Nine times out of ten the women involved are gruesome and no real loss to the gene pool, but every now and then you do indeed come across a pavement ape with his arm draped around a girl of European descent who's genuinely attractive, and who really ought to be with someone better. Cathy is most definitely one of these better looking girls. God only knows what goes through the minds of such women, and why they do it. Attention? Masochism? Maybe they enjoy domestic violence, who knows? What I do know, however, is that it's an extremely taboo subject and that if I don't want to turn Ingrid away from me then I'd best pretend all's well with the world. "Best of luck to her," I find hard to say, "I'm sure it will be a beautiful baby." That almost killed me.

"Well, if he turns out anything like the father, he will at least be charismatic." The way she leaves it there, not to mention that she spoke of charisma and not aesthetics as I did, makes me question if there's something she's holding back. Like maybe she doesn't approve.

"Go on?" I can't help but prompt the girl.

She shrugs her slender, golden shoulders. "For me, the main issue is that Cathy will eventually leave this place and because Winston's pledged to stay, well, that means the child will be left fatherless like so many others. Anyway, it doesn't matter because it's all just speculation."

"No, it's not," Jimmy pipes up and retakes his seat, "I take it you haven't been watching the videos she posts to her hundred-thousand YouTube subscribers? She's quite open and shameless about the fact she's fucking the Rastafarian who's supposedly running this place."

Rupert blows out air. "And she looks so innocent." Indeed she does, with her blonde bob cut and angelic features, though women with curves like that tend to find themselves with options and women with options usually fuck. Rupert's having problems averting his gaze from the women's table, probably because this Cathy, even now, is looking a bit too comfortable sitting beside Milly, and if she turns out to be a bad influence, then…

"Ok then, so my original point stands, which means Cathy's child will almost certainly be left fatherless, and that's a horrible thought." Ingrid now gestures towards the door on the left. "At least with Gabriel and Marie the child will have a father…"

"Not biological!" Jimmy growls.

She makes a face as if to suggest she's having a conversation with a naughty schoolchild. "That shouldn't even matter, as long as Gabriel loves the child, that's all that counts and anyway," she reaches across the table to slap Jimmy on the grotesquely sunburned forearm, "you don't even know for sure that the rumours are true."

Jimmy rolls his eyes. "You cannot be serious."

She turns up her palms. "You saw how they are together, the Frenchies, they're crazy about each other. Do you really think Gabriel wants to share his wife with anyone?"

"And *you've* seen how often they're both in the boss's office-boudoir."

"That doesn't mean anything, Gabriel has an important job out in the village and Marie's in charge of the teaching staff."

"Right," Jimmy snorts, "that's what the three of them are doing at two in the fucking morning loud enough to wake everybody in the dormitory, discussing logistics and curriculums." He shakes his head. "You don't notice it because you're staying with old Mrs Tittie…"

"Well, I'll be the first to know since I'm the person delivering the baby, and it's pronounced Tet-tay! Anyway, Winston's already with Cathy…"

Laughing raucously, Jimmy tips so far back in his seat that I fear he's about to have an accident. "Oh, love, you're young and beautiful, but you've got a lot to learn, particularly when it comes to men, and black men at that," he said that last part under his breath, "not to mention women. Look, I've got work to be doing, so if you truly believe the next big shit Marie takes will have only French features then why don't you put your money where your mouth is?"

There's silence for a moment. "I don't have money to gamble."

"Nonsense, I've seen where you live on Facebook, and don't deny your dad owns that medical supplies company whose HQ takes up half of Stockholm." This prompts a gasp from her but she doesn't deny any of it. So Ingrid's loaded as well as supermodel attractive. Jimmy rubs his hands together. "But I'm not talking about money necessarily…"

Her beautifully trimmed eyebrows pull closer together. "Then what are you talking about?"

"Oh, I don't know," he throws his hands up in the air, "let's see, um, yeah … if that baby comes out black as the ace of spades then you have to give my friend Monty here a hand job."

There's a mixture of sniggers, snorts and laughter, while all I want to do is kill the Irish bastard. If I ever had a chance with Ingrid, which was highly debatable to begin with, then Jimmy's now all but killed it. Though like scoring four numbers in the lottery, although it's not going to change your life much, you still wouldn't turn down a hand job, especially if the girl the appendage is attached to happens to look like Britt Ekland in her prime.

"Very funny," I tell him as a bead of sweat rolls down the back of my neck. I turn to her. "Don't listen to him. As you said, he's just bitter because of Cathy."

Her face has turned red, I'm very keen to notice, though you can believe me when I say that I've also noted the way she hasn't recoiled at the mere suggestion. Maybe, by some strange quirk of nature, the girl doesn't find me completely fucking repellent like most of the others. She swipes the green braid out from her eyes. "And there was me thinking, Jimmy, that you were here on pastoral work experience." Oh, I like that answer.

He stands and pushes his seat back under the table with a thud. "Aye, well, the truth is that now I'm beginning to question my entire feckin vocation, and all it took was having to spend a few months with a bunch of narcissistic, snobby Western do-gooders." He points at Cathy, who's dancing with a bunch of children - whilst ensuring Greta's filming every moment of it, no doubt for her YouTube channel. "Do you see what I mean now, Monty?" He shakes his head and storms away.

The tension is thick because, at least for me, I'm still thinking about Ingrid's hand wrapped around my cock. We make eye contact and both flash the same uncomfortable smile.

And then the wails of Marie, deep in the throes of orgasm penetrate the walls.

CHAPTER 5

An Incident

MONTGOMERY

"So much drama over a man who might not even exist," Rupert remarks in the car on the way back to the resort.

Indeed, the boss didn't bother troubling himself to make an appearance outside of his lair our entire first day in Aburi, and there can be no denying the drama between what amounts to a bunch of "snobby Western do-gooders" is both comedic and tragic. It can't be easy for Jimmy, every day having to watch Cathy slinking out from that office door, her face flushed red and her hair all mussed as she carries a black baby around inside of her. Personally, I can very much understand why such a thing would rile him, the constant reminder of it, though I can't help but question how he'd allowed his emotions to get so out of control in the first place, given he's training to be a priest and the Catholic Church forbids sexual relations of any kind.

"Maybe it's the proximity?" Rupert had pondered during a private moment away from our Irish friend. "If you're used to seeing pretty red-headed women and then find yourself in a place like this..." he'd gestured around the village and there was no need to explain any further, "well, perhaps the lack of white flesh, along with the heat, has addled his brain."

I'd agreed wholeheartedly. "The bugger needs to get over it, and her! It's bad enough that she's already pregnant with another man's child, the fact it's one of *them* ought to put upon it the world's largest exclamation mark." Just talking about it had made the bile taste come up in my mouth. "No, Money, once you go black, we don't want you back. I only worry for any young, impressionable girls that whore's influencing with her dumb YouTube videos."

Rupert had said nothing, as I'd expected he wouldn't, though I did catch him silently nodding.

"Might not exist?" Now, it's Milly who jerks me out from my depressing reverie. "Of course Winston exists, we've *met* him, haven't we, Belle?"

The object of my desires hums in affirmation. "Yup, though I can't see what the fuss is about, personally." *Because you're one of the better ones, and I love you so deeply for it.*

"He's just a chilled out dude," Milly volunteers, "and women go for that in a man, you know, the strong, unflappable, silent type."

Rupert's giving her a queer look. "Yeah, alright, darling, I'm right here."

She turns to him and pinches his cheeks. "I don't think you've got anything to worry about, my perty-pert."

We roll into the resort, an evening of well-earned relaxation ahead, though I find myself already missing Ingrid's company. Undoubtedly, the ego boost was more than welcome, though I must be careful not to lose track of my true aims, namely, Arabella.

I've learned my lesson and this time I lather up with factor 100, despite the fact I still have absolutely zero intention of allowing the sun to even touch me. "Damn stuff's like custard…" and neither is my sore skin absorbing it. There's laughter from outside the bathroom and I twist around to find Belle covering her mouth with a hand.

"You … are you sure that's viscous enough for you?"

"Yeah, alright, I have to watch out for my skin, you know, and somehow I don't think that factor 20 you use will cut it. Say…" I angle my back around to face her and tap my shoulder, "I don't suppose you wouldn't mind…"

"Belle … you ready?" It's Milly who's shouting from the other room.

"Yeah, coming," Belle replies before dashing off.

"I'd have done it for you," I mutter, suddenly reminded I'm lugging around rancid fifteen-day-old semen. "Fuck, but what I wouldn't give to be allowed to rub lotion over you."

"It's really starting to sting now," I complain to Rupert about my sunburn as we all head down the beach towards the sun loungers, "I read it's supposed to stop hurting after five days." Truth is I'm not sure I can endure it for so long.

"I'll remember not to slap you with a wet towel."

"I appreciate that, friend." I've just remembered something. "Slow down, let those two walk in front." We let the girls get ahead and, of course, all I'm able to do is stare at Belle's arse in this yellow two-piece bikini she thought to torture me with today. Despite the arrival of Ingrid in my life, it's still Belle I long for, and the manner in which her peachy buttocks give way to an impossibly tiny waist is a reminder of precisely why, even if this new Swedish blonde would make an exceptional consolation prize. I manage to tear my eyes away from the slim strip of material that's hitched up Belle's crack in order to address the matter at hand. "So, big boy, how's the stealthing going?"

His silence speaks volumes. He lets out a groan.

"What?"

He's still sighing. "It's kind of embarrassing, Monty…"

"Come on now, you can tell me."

He pinches at the skin atop his nose. "Well, the thing is that yesterday, you know, after your little pep talk, I, um, kind of had a drink too many and by the time it came to bed I wasn't really in the mood."

My jaw clenches. "Damn it, I said get *her* drunk, not yourself."

He throws up his hands. "It's all too much, Monty, you're making me so nervous with all this … *stuff* … I'm expected to do, how am I possibly supposed to go through with it?"

"You couldn't even get it up, could you? Last night, I mean."

"Nerves will do that to a man!"

"Evidently, and apparently even when your bird looks like *that*!" I jab a finger in the direction of his incredibly attractive and awesome red-headed girlfriend who might well soon be travelling the world with her dance troupe, after all. I'm squinting hard at him now. "Can I ask you something?"

"You're going to anyway."

"When did the two of you … last…?"

He looks suddenly down into the sand, ashamed.

My mouth plunges open of its own accord. "When, Rupert?"

"We've done it!" He's quick to blurt out, defensively. "But she tells me the act of intercourse causes her too much pain, and…" he trails off, hopeless. "Though she's exceptionally charitable with her hand, that I will say." Shit! It's all coming out now, and I almost regret asking.

"Pain?" I hiss. I've seen what Rupert packs after that time he mistakenly sent a dick pic to me instead of Milly, and you can trust me when I say that thing ain't causing pain to any woman. "You've been dating three years," I say incredulously, "the last two of which you've shared a student flat in Oxford. Buddy, when did the two of you last fuck?"

His shoulders slump forwards. "About six months ago." And although I'm not cruel enough to ask how *that* went, I'm betting it was entirely for the sake of appearances.

I let out an involuntary exhalation. Of course, for Milly, a girl from an average family in Sunderland, there are advantages that come from dating the son of one of the richest landowners in England, for example, having your rent paid, trips to Amsterdam, the pyramids, Bora Bora, skiing last winter in Sweden, all things which would otherwise be unattainable for Milly, not to mention the ring that Rupert's planning to bestow upon her this trip. He's given her everything, though apparently, mind blowing sex ain't one of them. Not for the lack of trying, I'm certain. Now, I can't say for sure that I can hold Milly in the same esteem as I did before, given I'm beginning to suspect she's only dating Rupert for the material goodies that come as part of the package. I just hope I'm wrong about that. Maybe I am. I mean, Rupert, not to mention his great many irritating foibles, are a lot to endure if you feel nothing for him physically.

Now, I can't help but think about our carefully laid plans to get her pregnant and that such a task might not be quite so easy as I'd originally hoped. "So let me get this straight ... you've not rutted once in the last six months?"

He shakes his head sadly. "Haven't you noticed the angst between us lately?"

"Quite honestly, my hapless friend, I don't pay the pair of you that much attention." I place my hand on his elbow, bringing us both to a stop. "Look, it's not the end of the world," I'm not sounding very convincing, even to myself, "focus, Rupert, focus! By my reckoning her most fertile days are today through Thursday, though you'll likely have one final shot on Friday to blow your filthy wad inside her muff."

"But Monty, if my size hurts her..."

I roll my eyes. "Forget that. You'll have to wine and dine

her, starting tonight, get her in the mood, munch that cunt until she's screaming for it, do you understand me?"

"What, you mean on top of everything else … the stealthing … how am I supposed to remem…"

"Dirty talk, go for a walk in public and smooch behind a wall, all daring like, tell her what you're going to do to her when you get back inside, hold her hand and feel up her tit with your elbow. That'll turn her on without her even knowing why." All things I'm intending to do with Belle just as soon as I get the chance. "Look, no alcohol today, alright? No, on second thoughts, maybe a couple of drinks might do you good, just to take the edge off, but no more than that, but get *her* bloody drunk, do you understand me?"

His shoulders go all limp. "I do hate having to do this."

"And you'll hate having to Insta-stalk her from a distance while she's partying up with her fellow dancers even more."

We catch up with the others and order cocktails, and of the four sun loungers I notice how the girls have occupied the two in the centre so that Rupert can lay beside his woman, which leaves the last remaining seat beside Arabella for me. I'm wearing my sunglasses so whilst taking position I'm able to ogle the girl without her knowing. She's lying back and I'm astonished by the way that even gravity struggles to flatten her breasts against her chest as so often happens when women recline back. She's ample, sports have made her wonderfully perky, and her bikini top is pushing the large globes together in such a way that I could quite easily lose my entire hand down the crevice. I shudder at the thought of burying my face in that deep cleft and inhaling so profoundly that I pass out, of flicking her nipples with my tongue, of putting a child inside of her so that they swell even more.

"It'll happen," I have to encourage myself, "slow progress." It's only now that I notice she's been watching me from above the rim of her sunglasses.

"Are you not taking off your jacket?" She blinks. "You'll suffocate in that thing."

"Right," I nod and reluctantly discard the garment. I lie back, cram the AirPods into my ears, close my eyes and blast out some Mozart. At some stage I fall asleep and eventually shake to, coming to a sitting position. Rupert and Milly are now strolling through the surf hand in hand, which means I'm now alone with the love of *my* life. Time to put on some moves, I clap my hands together, twist around to my right and find Belle now facing down with two large black hands massaging her shoulders.

"What the fu…" I yank out the AirPods and can only stare with an open mouth at the intruder.

"Ah, Monty, my friend, and how are you today?" Kojo manages to spare me a grin from his seated position, right there with his knees planted either side of Belle's buttocks as my eyes can only fix on her bear back, the bikini top having been removed to attenuate the tan line. Or did he remove it? Or she for him? Either way, the contrast in colours couldn't be more severe as he kneads the muscles beneath her supple flesh. Belle's facing me, my sudden awakening not exciting her in the least, her eyes are closed and the sides of her mouth are turned up into a relaxed smile.

I haven't forgotten about Kojo's actions last night when, on top of everything else, he almost certainly attempted to poison me so that he could have a clear run at Belle. I glance towards the ocean and the children playing in the shallows, and then back to Kojo as the dense, black musculature of his pectorals twitch from the effort of squeezing my soon-to-be woman's back. How has he not yet been fired for negligence? I'm beginning to suspect this country, along with its people, are hardly sticklers for duty or much else besides.

Kojo reaches down towards the sand and returns with a bottle of factor 20, squirts a dollop into his hands and then rubs it into the area between Belle's shoulder blades.

I let out an audible snort but nobody seems to notice. So this big, dopey African's using the guise of protecting Belle's skin to feel her up. This girlfriend and wedding story of his has to be complete bullshit, I'd bet my life on it. Recalling the selfie I took with Rupert last night, some small, vague idea begins to form in my head, maybe for later, just in case, because you never know, and so covertly I take out my phone and video the shocking spectacle for as long as I dare, maybe ten seconds or so before stuffing it back inside my bag.

"Belle?" I cough into a closed fist. "Do you fancy coming in for a dip?"

"Hmmm," she hums in the sort of way that almost reminds me of women in pornos when a large man first enters her after a half hour of agonizing foreplay, "no, you go ahead."

Damn. I'm not sure what to do now. If I go on my own then I'm leaving him alone with her. But neither can I stay now that I've made the offer, otherwise I'll look even more like a puppy dog than I already do. I glance anxiously again towards the ocean…

And as so often happens when my back's against the wall, the inspiration finds me. I know exactly how to expose Kojo, and quite possibly get him fired into the bargain. "Fine," I say loud enough to make a point, "I'll go on my own."

I stomp off down the sand, discard my flip-flops, throw off my vest, bypass a bunch of kids and splash into the shallows. The water's cool, a wonderful contrast against the heat as I wade further in and a few seconds later the waterline's up to my waist. I start to swim out, though obviously not too far, before twisting around and bobbing up and down, fixing my eyes on Kojo and Belle.

They're both sitting facing each other now, the African having taken Milly's seat, and I don't like the way they're both leaning closer to converse. They don't know I'm watching them, watching very intently indeed, and my heart beats hard as I'm able to observe, to see what they do whilst they believe they can get away with it. Something brushes against my foot but I kick it away. I continue spying. Belle tips back to laugh at something he says. Kojo flexes his bicep and Belle reaches forwards to give it a squeeze. He prods up his sunglasses. Gesticulates for some reason. She flexes her bicep and he reaches forwards to feel her up in turn. He nods. Makes a bench pressing motion. There's a gym on this resort. If Belle likes muscles then perhaps I should make more of an effort to get myself into shape. Build myself up. Better body. Better man. Someone worthy of a girl like Arabella. Not, I silently concede, some creep who spies on her from a distance. I sigh. "What the fuck am I even doing? I'm better than this!"

Kojo's hand touches her knee. Fuck him! Shouldn't he be keeping an eye on his patch? Time to go with the plan.

"Help!" I yelp. "Help!" I splash about the place, flap my arms, taste salt, make a fuss. The nearby kids stop and stare but neither Kojo nor Belle have even noticed. "Heeeeelllllppppp!" Oh, you stupid son-of-a-bitch, Kojo, don't pretend you can't hear me, when the truth is you're a work-shy bastard who won't, or can't, do his job.

Something touches my foot again, slips around, nestles against me, so I kick it away. It persists so I kick harder and am immediately assailed by a horrendous cramp spasming through my entire leg. I tense up, unable to move, bloody, fucking long day digging trenches without stretching has done this, no doubt about it. My teeth clench together and I plunge beneath the surface, swallow a lungful of seawater and bob back up, gulp a breath of air and once again fall below. I manage to heave myself above again, scream with everything I have, through the encroaching haze manage to see the kids pointing, shouting in my direction. I scream again but it's drowned out by the crash of rolling waves. Again, I fall beneath, my world turns dark, empty, and the next thing I know I'm being cradled in strong black arms. Again, the world turns dark and I don't know when next I open my eyes but when I do I'm lying faced up on the sand, a crowd of people all looking down, blocking out the sun above.

"Thank God, mate, are you alright?"

"Thought we lost you…"

"Lucky we had Kojo."

"Was dreading having to call your mum."

I cough vile sea water over my neck and chest. "What happened?" I just manage to croak, unsure if the blurry image of Belle with her arm thread tightly inside the crook of a grinning Kojo's elbow is real or not.

"To Kojo!" Everybody cheers and under the circumstances I feel compelled to enthusiastically clink champagne glasses with everyone.

Tonight's all on me, as it's hard not to treat the man who saved your life to a slap-up meal, especially when everybody else is insisting you must, though I can't help but grimace when the big guy orders the fillet steak, having already devoured a huge platter of cold cuts for starters. The man likes his meat. Big surprise there. But after the monumental fuck up that was today, why not add to the ever-growing list of misfortunes spending half your allowance feeding your potential love rival.

We're at La Piccola Casa, one of the resort's restaurants and Kojo, being the guest of honour, chose to sit himself between Belle and myself.

"My two favourite English people." He places his arms around the both of us and I feel the tension, as well as inhale some musky African scent, when he tugs us closer into his chest. I manage to pull back but Belle's hand is still pressing against him, her eyes closed as her face nestles into that area where his shoulder meets his pectoral. Finally, he lets go and I resist the temptation to rub the moisture from my cheek.

"More champagne," Kojo says to the dark-skinned waiter and I'm starting to become so paranoid that I can't help but question whether a certain knowing glance is exchanged between the two employees of the White Sands Beach Resort, as in, *oh no, not another European sex tourist come to sample some of the local dark delicacies, wink wink, and look at this poor hapless white fool who thinks he's in with a shot, she's about to get stuffed more than she ever has and this ginger imbecile's paying for it all, hahahaha.* Kojo points to a bottle near the bottom of the menu and I dare not look at the price. "We will have this one, Cedric."

I touch Kojo's arm and feel the solid musculature beneath the white shirt he bothered wearing for the occasion. "Say, I don't suppose you get the staff discount?"

Before he can even answer, a tall brunette in her late thirties is making a beeline for our table. I instantly recognize her as the buxom white sex tourist I'd seen on the beach yesterday getting her toes massaged by a particularly large and nasty black brute. She leans down between myself and the African and I get an instant whiff of aloe vera, almond and baobab, reminding me of that balm black people back home like to rub all over themselves. She faces him and Belle, cutting me off from the exchange entirely.

"Why, hello there," she sounds German and places her hand on Kojo's shoulder, "I just wanted to come over and say that I think it was amazing what you did earlier," Belle, I notice, has crossed her arms and is giving the evil eye to the woman, but the newcomer sees this and attempts to disarm the object of my desires by reaching over Kojo and, in turn, touching her on the forearm, "and you, my dear, are the luckiest girl in the world."

Even though the woman has made an incorrect assumption, thank God, the acknowledgement that she recognizes, at least to her mind, that the two of them are dating now serves to disarm Belle entirely. Belle uncrosses her arms as her expression softens immensely, and that she doesn't immediately set the woman straight is both telling and alarming.

I'm quick to loudly interject, "they're not..." I'm cut off when the woman's hip wallops into me.

Her hand is back on Kojo's shoulder. "Well, if you ever get tired of this pretty one then come find me," she says in such a way as to make it clear it's obviously a joke, even though there can be little doubting she'd love nothing more than to take him back to her chalet for a tumble along with the other one she's leading on with promises of transportation back to the Rhineland. Belle knows this too, of course, and although she's now relaxed her posture, it's easy to see that all she wants to do is jab a fork through the woman's eyeball.

I interrupt with, "why not tonight? There's nothing stopping the pair of you from..."

Now she twists around on me. "And you, you silly boy," her tone reminds me of how a school teacher might address a particularly bothersome child as she looks at me with what can only be described as complete contempt, "maybe next time you decide on wading into the ocean you'll remember your rubber ring and armbands."

There are various snorts from all present, Belle included, even Rupert, and when finally she walks away I'm promising myself that should I ever happen to see the slut again then I'm seriously going to throw sand in her face.

I'm pissed off because from all the dating material I've read I happen to know there's nothing that turns women onto men more than seeing other women showing interest in them. It's that whole infuriating social proof thing that only demonstrates the ridiculous herd mentality of most women. Not only that, but the inverse would be being seen to receive another woman's contempt and ridicule, which I most certainly just did, and that could only knock me down yet further in Belle's mind. "Fucking cunt!" I snarl at her back when she's walking away.

"Hey, you, enough of that," it's Milly whose hand lightly slaps my own atop the table, "you did go out beyond what was safe for someone who can't swim."

"I keep telling you," I growl, "I *can* swim! I got cramp from all the digging."

"Well then, you should have stretched before swimming out there, shouldn't you." Now it's Belle who's piling in. "I mean, it's basic common sense."

"Hey, give my friend Monty a break," it's Kojo whose arm is back around my shoulders and I can't help but feel like a child, physically, every time he does this, "if it was not for people swimming out beyond their capabilities, I would be out of a job."

"See!" I say a little too quick before realizing there might have been a veiled put down contained in his words, although to look at the man's poker face it's hard to tell if there was any malice intended.

The subject is forgotten when the food arrives and because I'm turning over a new leaf, and also because I'm paying, I ordered the salad. Milly, I note, is on her third glass of champagne, Rupert sticking with the Coke so that things tonight, for a fucking change, might go according to plan.

There's something I've been waiting to throw out there, just to see the reactions, so here goes... "Such a pleasant meal, I'm really happy we did this, truly," I top up Milly's champagne glass, "say, Kojo, you should have brought along your fiancée. I'd have been more than happy to spend my money on her too."

Perhaps knowing that I'm scheming something, Rupert's jaw jerks knowingly towards me, Milly, who's none the wiser about anything perks towards Kojo for his answer but Belle, who you can bet I'm watching closer than anyone else, is conspicuous by her complete lack of any reaction at all, which irks me as it should. Indeed, she merely persists with the job of cutting into her fish, though I can tell her ears are poised for whatever information is about to be conveyed.

Kojo, if indeed as I suspect he's wanting only to defile the flesh of innocent white tourists, should right now on cue squirm and wriggle and shrivel and turn the blackest shade of red you ever saw, now that he's been so cleverly exposed. "That is very kind of you, Monty, my friend, but Ashantay must stay home to look after her sick mother."

There are only sympathetic moans from everybody present and infuriatingly, Belle runs her hands down Kojo's arm to show her support, being sure to give the biceps a little squeeze as she does.

Why is it that all my attempts to show the man in his true light only end up bringing them closer together? Does she even care that he's engaged to be married, or so he says? Maybe it's that social proof thing again, that because another woman has already tied him down, apparently, that now she sees Kojo as a challenge. You see what I mean, dear reader? I'm right here, single, ready and waiting, and yet she's feeling up this African she's only known ten minutes instead of the man who's spent the last five years absolutely besotted with her. It makes no sense. And assuming my fears are justified, where could it possibly lead? He lives and works in Ghana. Is she seriously willing to burn her bridges with me, her potential future boss as well as husband, just for a holiday fling with this low-IQ savage?

"They're just friends," Rupert reassures me on the walk back to the chalet, "and it's because of how you feel for her that you're blowing every little thing up out of all proportion."

I grunt. Perhaps there is some truth to that. At least there'd better be.

"And she happens to be a touchy-feely person, so that kind of behaviour is to be expected."

I'm not so sure that's true. Not once has she ever been so touchy-feely with me.

"Anyway," Rupert continues, "if it makes you feel better, next time we'll find a patch of beach far away from him and relax there. Done! Easy as that."

"I hope so, the man's seriously getting in my way."

Rupert throws up an arm, stops and whips around on me. "Mate, Belle's not a nasty fucking coal burner, alright? She's one of the best women I've ever known!"

I'm taken aback by his sudden ferocity and step away from him with my hands raised defensively. "Ok, ok, calm down. I know. What's gotten into you?"

There's a bench nearby and he almost collapses into it before slumping forwards and balling into his hands.

I sit beside him, uncomfortable. "Rupert, tell me." What the fuck is it this time? I'm almost afraid to ask.

It takes a minute for him to start talking. "When you were asleep before," he begins through palpitations, "Milly and I took a walk along the beach and she told me how excited she was to be starting with the London Festival Opera."

"Right…"

"Monty, I asked her what she thought it would mean for *us*…"

"Well, that was a stupid thing to do. You don't ask her anything, we're deciding this *for* her, remember…"

"She said she loves me but that she also thinks the distance will be a challenge for us going forward."

"Well, duuuuurrr, we already knew that, which is precisely why you need to…"

"Monty, don't you get it? She's choosing the stupid opera thing over me…"

"As I suspected she would…"

He gives me a look and I almost fear he's about to pulverize me.

I soften my face. "Look, Rupert, this doesn't change anything, and it certainly doesn't alter our plan or what you need to do." I glance to my left for the girls who're walking behind us, their two silhouettes are a couple of minutes away. "Listen, don't let Milly catch you like this. You need to dry your face and turn on your seduction mode." However the fuck that might look.

He splutters tears. "Don't worry, it's not happening tonight, not after the quarrel we had. She never lets me touch her after a falling out." Nor, apparently, at any other time either. My hand balls into a fist. He continues, "didn't you notice the friction between us at dinner?"

"No," I hiss.

I let out a loud exhalation. "Look, it's not good, but neither is it the end of the world. So that's two days out of four, possibly five that you've squandered, which means you've got another two, maybe three shots at keeping her forever." At least with regards this egg. There'll be one more after this and then that's it, gone forever. I pat him reassuringly on the back. "Don't worry, there's absolutely nothing to worry about."

Unless, of course, my hapless friend finds yet another way to fuck everything up.

CHAPTER 6

Two Transactions

MONTGOMERY

Not wanting to fuck things up myself, I rouse early next morning determined that this fresh start thing I'm doing will work out, which is why now I'm heading for a workout. Even if, God forbid, my Arabella dreams don't come true then at least by putting on some muscle I'll be more enticing to the consolation prize, Ingrid.

After finding the gym, I change into my shorts and a sleeveless vest before spending a moment surveying my image in the changing room mirror. I'm average height, perhaps a little shorter, which is fair enough, but I'm not happy about the paunch I've developed over five years drinking most nights whilst studying fine art. I've never been happy with my skinny arms, nor the tiny muscle that appears when I dare to flex. My upper body sags back, which makes my belly project forwards even worse, and gives the overall appearance of terrible posture. "Thank God I've got money." Yes, thank God for that.

I enter the gym and am immediately struck by the dark lighting, stuffy atmosphere, lack of cardio machines, and the abundance of weights benches and free weights. Definitely a muscle head's gym. The sweaty stink is overwhelming, despite the fact it's early and there's only one other guy present, oh, and his woman, which happens to be the annoying mudshark from the restaurant last night.

He notices the scrawny ginger immediately, makes a double-take, and I hear the snort from across the room. He's absolutely enormous, one of those roid-soaked black freaks with veins popping out all over the place and who can barely move for all his bulk. He wears baggy clothing out of necessity. He carefully works the bar with five heavy plates either side onto his shoulders and as he does his upper back muscles bulge obscenely. The ridiculous weight now supported, he squats down and I almost fear he's about to get crushed beneath the load. He lets out a shout as he pushes upwards, the weight successfully lifted, and then repeats the process several more times before re-racking the straining bar.

I swallow back a mouthful of saliva and remember my new leaf before daring to approach the man where he now sits resting his quads. "Um," I cough into a closed fist, "I ... I don't suppose you would happen to have any, um, assistance?"

He looks slowly up and a long stream of sweat pours down the side of his face. "Whut?"

"Um, chem…chemical assistance."

"You mean roids, little white man?" In just barely visible wisps, steam rises from Milky's neck.

"Sure," I rub the back of my neck and feel like a seventeen-year-old attempting to illegally purchase his first beer at the pub, "preferably something that works fast." I glance to my right, to where the self-hating swirler's setting up her phone to take a video of her next set of barbell squats, no doubt for her Instagram, or whatever. I subconsciously make a half step to the side in the hopes I'll be out of the picture, unlikely as it will be, though I'll settle gladly with her not coming over here to engage.

The brute delves into his bag resting beneath the bench. "First time," he states matter of fact, because duurr, and pulls out a small vial, "Testosterone Cypionate."

I suck in air. "I…I was hoping for something edible, like a pill, or something."

Milky's enormous nostrils flare with annoyance, probably because I'm keeping him from his next set. "It is like this." He now pulls out a bagful of syringes and tosses them onto the bench beside his enormous rump, his every movement slow and constrained by his mass. "You will need to inject it into your buttocks."

I'm already reconsidering this but then I remember Belle and the way she's always squeezing Kojo's arms. "How often?"

"Every other day, but you still have to train hard and eat right, or else you are wasting your time." His voice is of that thick-gummed African type you always need a while to make sense of.

I nod. "How much?"

He considers me for a moment. "For this, hundred dollars, American, and I will give you the syringes."

Hmm, it still sounds a little steep, but it's not like there are any other steroid dealers in the vicinity. No, this guy has the market cornered, at least here, so he can probably charge what he wants. I pull out my wallet and he raises his chin to peer upwards at the bills poking out.

"Make that two hundred."

"What? No way, you said…"

He stands, which is about all he needs to do for me to succumb at once.

"Ok, ok, two hundred." I snatch out the money and quickly hand it over, grabbing the vial and syringes. "How long until I see results?" I've definitely been mugged, in a way.

He'd been in the process of turning away but slowly twists

back, only irritation upon his grotesque features. "A week to see some early gains, if you train hard, eat right. A month for the real results to kick in."

It could be better but I'll take it. Being a novice, I'm quite self-conscious to start lifting shit in front of this enormous guy, and I haven't a fucking clue what I'm doing anyway, but I decide to train first and then inject the chemicals when I'm done, just on the off chance I absolutely hate lifting weights and decide never to come back; I have bitch tits already, thanks. I'm sure there'll be side effects but nothing that outweighs the prospect of losing Belle to one of these cavemen.

Luckily, the ridiculous couple leave a few minutes after our transaction, which means there's now an empty gym to make a fool of myself, which was the reason I came early before we have to leave for Aburi. I go to the bench press and start by lifting an empty bar, slowly adding the lighter plates to each side. When that's done I try the lat pulldown, some barbell squats and finish with some bicep curls. By the end I'm exhausted and head back to the changing rooms, find an empty stall and perch on the throne. I take the vial from my pocket and read the instructions. *"400mg per week?"* Milky said to inject every other day. "400mg every other day it is then."

I've never done anything like this before and the truth is I'm shaking as I unscrew the cap, dip the needle into the fluid and slowly draw a quantity of Testosterone Cypionate into the syringe. What does 400mg even look like? And there are no markers or indicators anywhere on this cheap fucking plastic syringe. Sod it. Am I supposed to do this sitting or standing? I shake it away. First time's usually the hardest when it comes to things like this. Next time will be easier. And what part of my arse? Left or right cheek? I'm stalling, I know I am. I grit my teeth, shut my eyes, reach around and stab myself, letting out a yelp that prompts whoever the fuck's taking a shit in the next stall to shuffle.

"Motherfucker!"

Gently, ever so gently, I press down on the plunger and once drained yank the thing out from my arse. I flush the toilet and exit. "That wasn't so bad." I take a breath and head for the urinal, pull myself free and let fly.

A shadow falls over me. "Hello, Monty, my friend," comes the deep voice as Kojo releases himself and commences to urinate right beside me.

"What the…" it's hard enough as it is, taking a piss whilst standing next to anyone, but try doing it when the man's a clear foot taller than you. In an instant, my strong, healthy stream diminishes to short spurts while Kojo sounds like he's spraying a fucking garden hose.

"It is another beautiful morning here at White Sands, I wish you only pleasantness for the day ahead." He casually glances to his right and down, and then his upper body makes a small backwards jerking motion.

"Wh…what?" I look down in turn and am dismayed to find my cock's shrivelled to something akin to a baby's toe, as I pinch it between my thumb and forefinger. Fuck! What happened? Is it the drugs or the fact I'm standing next to…

He looks away and is silent for a moment. "Yes, a beautiful morning here at…" he trails off awkwardly and shakes his head.

Being unable to help myself, I glance to my left and down, and make a similar small backwards jerking motion, though for a completely different fucking reason. I've read sub-Saharan Africans are showers, not growers, at least I hope that's the case because otherwise I'm in a great deal of trouble. Without staring too obviously, I try to decide if his flaccid is larger than my hard, or how my hard used to stand up before I started dabbling in anabolic steroids. He's definitely thicker. Uncut. I decide that he's probably not, though I also recognize I'm trying to make myself feel better. *They're just friends*, I have to remind myself, she'll put photos of herself on facebook looking all pally with the African so she can feel enlightened. Women do this shit all the time. They like to feel superior even though such behaviour fools nobody and anyone with any sense even looks down on it. Damn thing's like a fully ripened aubergine.

I will myself to refortify, if only to save face. "Yes, it's a beautiful…"

"I will see you later, Monty, my friend." He pats me on the back, leaving me alone to finish up and a couple of minutes later I'm exiting the building, red-faced and self-conscious.

Belle nearly breezes straight past me at the doors. "Oh, good morning," she stops suddenly, "I was wondering where you were." She's togged in a pair of yoga shorts and a sleeveless vest, a sight that makes me tremble with lust.

It's now sixteen days and counting weighing me down and I'm tempted to quickly crack one off just to make sure the thing's still working but no, instead I think about how good it will feel to finally position myself at Belle's entrance before pushing slowly inside of her, a full sack of jizz waiting to be deposited.

"Just went for an early morning…" my voice is coming out alarmingly high-pitched, she notices and her eyebrows pull closer together, "are you training with Kojo?" I sound accusatory.

Her eye twitches. "Not that it's any of your business, but yes, we arranged to train together last night." You see, dear reader, this is precisely why women must be kept on a tight leash at all times. She moves into her favourite arms akimbo position, all defiant, almost like she's daring me to complain about it.

I dare not, though I come pretty close. "Well don't forget we're leaving for Aburi in an hour."

"I won't. Is that all?"

I have nothing else, and now I'm going to be spending the next hour, indeed, the rest of the day and beyond wondering what the fuck they're doing. "I'll see you in the car." I head off but then turn around again so that I can stare at her arse in those shorts as she stomps away.

It's not good. I hate feeling so helpless about it, about her, that there's nothing I can do to make her notice me. It'll be a month, at least, before the steroids kick in, but the way things are going she'll be permanently tainted by this African long before then. No, there has to be something else I can do, something even more drastic than cheating to build up my body. I have an idea starting to take shape from within the darkest recesses of my brain, though it's such a do-or-die option that I really don't want to even contemplate such a prospect unless it's absolutely necessary.

What I didn't know then was that taking such drastic measures was soon to be forced upon me.

<hr>

It's whilst attempting to dislodge with my shovel what's almost certainly a human femur that my day is ruined yet further when I hear the second-hand information, through Rupert via Milly, that Belle has arranged to meet Kojo at the resort bar this evening.

"It's a date! It's a fucking date!" I'm grabbing Rupert by the shirt collar as my entire body feels numb.

"I hate to admit it," Rupert begins, "but it's not looking good."

I smile sarcastically. "And it was only last night you were so insistent she's not a lousy fucking coal burner."

"Well … it *could* be innocent?"

"Am I really supposed to take that chance?" I smash at the femur with the shovel. "Fucking break!"

"Probably not."

Jimmy, standing a short way off, shields his eyes from the sun to glance in our direction. "What are you two yammering about? Get back to work."

I ignore him. "I'm going to have to do something about this."

"You are the ideas man." He shrugs. "To be honest, I'm rather surprised you haven't already nipped this in the bud."

That prompts a bark to escape me. My friend doesn't even know that it was me who orchestrated the downfall of Bradley, the last man who attempted to get close to Belle. But he's right! I've allowed this, whatever *this* is, to persist for far longer than I ought to have.

I check the time on my phone. It's eleven in the morning, which leaves more than enough time to make a short, unpleasant trip and return here before we have to leave for the resort. I tell Rupert to watch out for my text messages before having a short conversation with Jimmy.

He scratches at his burns. "Business in Accra? Are you feckin insane?"

I don't ask him what he'd be willing to pay to make it so that Cathy wasn't carrying around inside of her some dirty Rastafarian's bastard. I still have a chance to ensure nothing similar ever happens to Belle, perish the thought. "I won't be long. If anyone asks then tell them I'm helping Gabriel." I don't wait for a response, after all, these people have no authority over me, for whatever reason I'm paying to be here.

I dash for the Humvee and tell the driver to take me to Accra.

<hr>

MY MIND'S rapidly scouring for a way to cock-block Kojo and by the time we're entering the dismal Accra suburbs, I settle upon an idea to ensure everybody's joining Belle tonight at the bar.

I fire off quick messages to Rupert telling him to inform Milly that the two of us just happened to have already arranged going to the resort bar this night in order to watch the England football game on the big screen. A few dollars ought to persuade whoever's in charge to ensure the match is being shown on the big screen. There's no reason Belle shouldn't believe our presence to be completely normal and given that she almost certainly knows how I feel about her, and that I've also made her an offer of employment that might just be rescinded should she do anything daft, then I ought to expect her to be on her best behaviour with regards exotic lifeguards.

"Are you sure here?" The driver calls out with hesitation from in front. We're grinding through a suburb that goes by the name Kwame Nkrumah Circle, and that I'm even here just goes to show how desperate things are becoming. It's all litter-strewn concrete, mad driving, loud incessant horn honking and giant overpasses below which gather dozens of what I've learned the locals call *ashawo* standing around in short skirts and high heels.

I'M TOGGED in my England shirt, which luckily I'd brought along on the trip with me, and I'd even managed to filch one of the Aburi village kid's footballs as an additional prop. I'm sure some organized charity or other will replace it eventually.

The three of us enter the bar only a few minutes after Belle, and I make sure to be bouncing the ball off my bonce, all innocent like, as we saunter up to order drinks. She's leaning against the bar with a cocktail, no sign of Kojo yet, and the way her face freezes when her eyes pass over mine tells me all I need to know, and the confirmation of what I'd hoped to be paranoia is truly devastating. It's Bradley all over again, only worse, because this time I'm dealing with a filthy nigger, and somehow I doubt the cops in this country, not to mention all the retarded feminists on social media, would treat an allegation of sexual abuse in quite the same way as back home.

To make matters worse, not to mention confirm my fears all the more, Belle's wearing the most delectable white blouse I've ever clapped eyes on, and that's been left unbuttoned just enough to reveal the insides of her sumptuously plump cleavage; not too slutty but definitely not classy either. She plucks the hems closer together, concealing as much as she can as I approach.

"You here for the game too?" I ask her nonchalantly whilst signalling to the barman, some gangly black who can't take her eyes off my woman, "three beers, my good man," I slam down twenty American dollars, "and please ensure there are no interruptions to our beautiful game."

"Um, not really, no." She gives Milly a certain look that now has me questioning how much the girls are in on this together. Milly makes a small shrugging motion and rolls her eyes for Belle's benefit.

"There should be a couple of players making their international debuts," I tell Belle and take a sip of my beer whilst trying my hardest not to stare down her crevice, "I take it you're a Rangers fan, you know, coming from Scotland, or are you Celtic?"

"Ah, hello there, my English friends, and hello especially to my very best English friend, Monty." Kojo strides up wearing his usual three-quarter length khakis that display his bulging calves and a white shirt that looks like it might rip if he does so much as bend his elbow. He fist bumps Rupert and Milly before embracing me in such a way that drives half the air out from my lungs, enveloping me in his musky coconut scent and spilling beer down my sleeve. I don't know why I always get preferential treatment considering I'd like nothing more than to see him fired and removed permanently from the resort. Finally, he nods at Belle who prods a waiting cocktail in his direction.

"Well, ain't this nice," I declare, "the whole gang together for the match," I throw up the ball and attempt to do a couple of kick-ups but only end up sending it into a nearby table and spilling even more beer down my sleeve.

Kojo laughs. "Monty, I do believe your skills leave much to be desired."

I'd spent much of the day learning as much about Kojo as I could; thank you once again, Facebook. Starting with the White Sands Beach Resort, I soon found a picture of the lifeguard above the caption 'come meet our friendly members of staff.' Clicking on his profile, it didn't take long to discover he's twenty-seven years of age, has a diploma in nutrition from some worthless institution based in Accra and a couple of years back had placed second in the Man Ghana bodybuilding competition. What was most interesting, however, were the pictures of his fiancée. Yes, dear reader, she truly exists and the wedding is indeed scheduled for June, no word of a lie, which means we have a rat, an adulterer, a cheater on our hands here. Of course, ordinarily I couldn't give the slightest damn about such a thing, but when the woman he wants to commit adultery with happens to be Belle, well then, now I care a great deal.

Clicking on the girl's profile, I found a not unattractive woman, at least by African standards, shaking her arse at the camera in image after image whilst posing beside the man who, even now, is clinking glasses with a white woman (I wonder how such a thing might go down, if only she knew).

I'm quick with my phone to catch the snap and upon covertly reviewing the image note the way Kojo's visibly staring down Belle's blouse that appears to have once again mysteriously popped open, whilst she bites down on her bottom lip appearing all abashed. It's a lucky shot, for sure, and added to the two I already possess, well, it's almost like there's a story being told here, painful as it will soon be for someone else in addition to myself.

The game commences. We've taken seats at a large table as close to the noisy screen as we could get and you can bet I was quick to position myself between Kojo and Belle before spreading myself out and engaging the man in long, drawn-out conversations about football, a subject I actually know very little about, and a range of other enthralling topics; the exchange rate, visa process, import taxes and digging a shit ditch in Aburi. There can be no denying he's a friendly guy, and under different circumstances might even have been likeable enough, though overall he's more than a little dim-witted and lacks terribly in any knowledge of anything immediately outside of his comfort zone, namely bodybuilding and this resort.

There are around a hundred people now in the bar and the atmosphere's becoming rowdy. For about the tenth time, Belle gives me the evil eye, her arms permanently folded from where she sits next to Milly. Both girls look bored out of their little minds, though Rupert, because he's my buddy and is eager to help me out here, is chipping in with the occasional anecdote, even if they're mostly lost on Kojo.

I try to be discreet about it but for about the twelfth time in as many minutes, I check the time on my phone. The entertainment's late. I can only blame myself. I know what these people are like and should have thought to book her for earlier than needed.

The match ends in a dismal 0-0 draw, though that's beside the point completely. Now, there's a moment of awkward silence where nobody seems to know what's happening next.

"Kojo," Belle says with a knowing tone, "would you like to accompany me to the bar?"

I'm quick to jump in. "Aye, that's a great idea, let's all go and grab some more drinks."

Her face clams up in the sort of way that all but confirms it, what I'm up against here. *She* might be hell-bent only on defiling herself but lucky for Belle there are some of us around here who are set on saving her. Unfortunately, as we all stand I'm powerless to prevent her from shoving me aside so that she can thread her arm inside of Kojo's. Rupert and I share a look and I've no doubt he can see the dismay on my features.

"Play it cool," he reminds me, which is why I allow the two of them some room at the bar, and I spend the next twenty minutes constantly checking the time whilst Kojo enthrals Belle with words I can't even hear, the odd gesticulation indicating that they're either talking about martial arts, racket sports or arse slapping whilst fucking doggy-style.

"Are you alright?" Milly asks.

"Huh?"

"I've never seen you looking so agitated." She moves into the space between Rupert and myself, cutting him off from the conversation and softens her angelic face. "I know you like her..."

"Who?" I say defiantly.

She rolls her eyes. "It's bloody obvious. I know it, you know it, and she knows it." She rubs my arm, a sympathetic gesture if ever there was one. "It's really sweet and all, but don't you think you're wasting your ... I mean, I don't want to sound harsh, but as a friend, I should probably tell you that I think Belle's just a little bit out of your league."

"What?" I can only hiss. I mean, I know all this full well, of course, but to actually hear it from Milly is like a dagger to the heart.

"And besides," she continues, "I think it's fairly obvious there's someone else she really..."

"Kojo!" Finally, the hooker I ordered strides straight up to the motherfucker, spinning him around by the arm and giving Belle the most hostile glare you could ever imagine. "You said there was nobody else but me and your fiancée!" Wow, she actually delivers the line better than I could ever have hoped.

I gasp exaggeratedly. "Oh, gosh, what a rat he turned out to be, and to think we allowed him into our company, our hearts."

Kojo takes a step back. "What is this?"

The hooker, who goes by the name Delight, was the nastiest, oldest, most shrivelled and least reserved I could find congregating under that bridge. In fact, she'd taken one look at me, some rich white guy looking for fun, supposedly, and had threatened all her grasping friends with what looked like a stocking filled with pebbles. Now, she slaps Kojo on the chest, which makes a dull thud against his hefty pectoral. "You promised me." The street walker's wearing black heels and a red dress that's so short you can almost see her wizard's sleeve vagina.

Rupert shakes his head. "This is very disappointing, tut-tut." Milly shushes him.

"Kojo, who is this woman?" Belle, contrary to what I'd hoped, is actually clinging to him in solidarity.

The lady of the night slaps him again. "The other evening when we fucked in the loading bay, you promised you would end things with all the others."

"And in a country so riven with AIDS..." I add, helpfully.

She turns to Belle. "Is this her, the tramp?"

"Tramp?" Belle dares step into her face. "You can talk, you nasty little bitch." Bloody hell. Nearly everyone in the bar's staring now.

"I think that my friend Benjamin has played a trick on me." Kojo tips back and lets out a raucous laugh. "Very good. I will be sure to get him back for this one."

To make matters even worse, now Belle's laughing. "Wow,

you sure are popular with the ladies." She casually slides an arm around the wide expanse of his back.

"I can't help it."

I grit my teeth and growl, "so he's arrogant too."

"Well, he can back it up," Milly says from close by and I cringe because she wasn't meant to hear that.

Delight's heels clap against the tiles as she approaches me, much to my alarm. "You pay now."

"Shit!" My balls suck closer to my arsehole, and I'm quick to rifle through my wallet and stuff a quantity of notes into her black fingers without even stopping to check how much. "Now, fuck off!" Mercifully, she does.

Milly squints at me. "What was that about?"

"She was, um, soliciting business and I told her to get lost."

"Then why did you give her money?"

"Um, I paid her to get lost, obviously." I turn away to the bar and console myself in my beer. All the more reason because a slow song has begun and Belle drags Kojo away to dance. "That's two fucking plans gone to shit."

Rupert's staying away, he knows my moods, but Milly leans against the bar and places a comforting arm around my back, and I have to admit that this is the closest I've come to crying since that appalling night I saw Belle and Bradley smooching beneath that tree.

"There are others," Milly soothes, "it's silly to pin all your hopes on one girl."

The beer shivers from within the glass. "Third time lucky."

"Excuse me?"

"I'm going to take a piss." I leave her and approach Rupert. "Take a video of them and send it to me. Now!" I storm out, find the toilets and lock myself inside a cubicle.

When I said 'third time lucky,' there are actually two parts to this final, last-ditch effort at saving everything; one to break Kojo down, another to build myself up. The former I've been collecting evidence for since day one, albeit not with a great deal of intention until now. The latter struck the bowels of my mind only this morning after speaking with Milky at the gym, and is something I'm willing to contemplate only now that the situation has become truly dire.

My phone vibrates, a message from Rupert, and I open the video to find Belle with her arms around Kojo's neck as they slow dance to Eric Clapton's Wonderful Tonight, his black hands clutching hard at her hips like some pre-sex ritual playing out before my blearing eyes. The final piece of evidence. Belle appears to tilt her jaw up for the kiss but it's actually Kojo who leans away and pulls apart before walking her back to the bar.

I edit that part out.

I then find Ashantay on Facebook and type the message. 'Hello, you don't know me, but I know your boyfriend Kojo. As a concerned Christian, I thought best that you should know about his recent antics here at the White Sands Beach Resort. Best of luck, whatever you decide to do.'

I attach the video with all the images and press send.

"WHERE'S KOJO?" I ask the gang after returning to the bar a few minutes later.

Everybody's finishing off the last of their drinks ready to leave. It's Belle who answers, looking beautifully dejected, not to mention rejected. "Dunno. He got a call and rushed away real quick."

"He didn't even say goodnight," Milly adds.

My eyebrows are quick to perk at this wonderful news. Wow. That didn't take long at all. "Back to the chalet then?" There's still champagne in the refrigerator.

The girls nod and lead the way. I place an arm athwart Rupert's sternum to slow his advance so that we can walk some distance behind and as the cool ocean breeze splashes across my face, I tell Rupert what I've done, if only so he knows not to blunder out any information with regards the video.

"Crikey, Monty, I hope that wasn't taking things a step far?"

"A step far?" I ask incredulously. "If I hadn't pushed the nuclear button then even now there might be an enormous nigger cock buried deep inside of my beautiful…" I can't even bring myself to finish the words, so appalling is the prospect.

"You know, hard as it is to believe, I'm not even sure if he's all that interested in her." Rupert absolutely says.

"Are you insane?"

He shakes his head. "I was watching them, probably more so than you were, in fact. You know, friend, perhaps I'm not quite so hopeless when it comes to certain things as you seem to think I am. I mean, if anything, she seems more interested in him than he does in her." Even if true, which I highly doubt, it's still incredibly fucking bad.

"You are insane. No dark-skinned savage would refuse the advances of any white woman, least of all a woman like Arabella."

"And yet that's precisely what happened. Didn't you watch the video?"

There's no need to tell him I edited that part out so instead I just grunt in affirmation. "I … I must admit, I'm not sure quite what to make of that." Indeed, it is hard to explain.

"Kojo's engaged, you said, and a Christian, so perhaps he takes these things a little more seriously than you give him credit for." Rupert makes an odd barking noise. "Perhaps we were both worried over nothing."

"He's still getting in my way." I kick at a pebble and watch as it skids across the concrete. "And besides, even if you're right, I'm still not taking any chances." Which brings me now to the other thing. "Listen, there's something important I have to do in the morning. Remember that favour you owe me?"

He nods and answers ominously, "yes."

"I'll almost certainly be calling it in."

"Gosh, Monty, calling it in? What is it you want me to do?"

I shake my head. "Tomorrow."

NEXT MORNING I arrive at the gym around the same time. If there's one thing about these muscle heads, it's that they spend time lifting weights, they're disciplined and have regular hours. I'm not surprised to find Milky, the big black brute is present, bench pressing a phenomenal amount of weight, his white whore again working on her ass. That's another thing about these people, black men, that is, they love their big booties.

I wait until he returns the bar to the hooks before approaching. "Good morning."

He attempts to use a towel to wipe the sweat from the back of his neck but his muscles are so large, and his flexibility so bad, that he's unable to stretch anywhere near that far behind himself. The size of his biceps also prevent the man from adequately closing the angle of his elbow. God only knows how he manages to wipe his arse. "No refunds."

I raise my hands into a defensive stance. "That's not what I want."

"Then what do you want." His stench is stinging and all-encompassing.

I'd given this more thought overnight. Even on the walk over, I was still thinking about what I was intending to do. It's probably not quite as bad as paying a girl to accuse a rival of sexual assault, so this not being the worst thing I've ever done in my life makes it easier. What pushed me over the edge is that I believe it to be necessary, unfortunately, because nothing else seems to be working. I take a breath and steady my heart. "I'd like to make you an offer."

"Whut?"

I steel myself to move closer and tell the brute exactly what I'd like him to do, at what time, and to who.

"You got a picture?" He asks.

I nod and pull out my phone, my hands are shaking as I press my thumb against the Touch ID, and I show him a photo of Belle in her Cambridge rowing jersey.

His fat lips pucker and he lingers for a while on the image. "I can see why you going to so much trouble."

"You won't mistake her for anybody else, that's for sure." I put the phone back in my pocket. "How much?" I've considered it most likely that the kind of guy who would as good as mug me whilst selling anabolic steroids might also be the kind of guy who'd be willing to do what I'm asking.

He strokes his jaw for a few moments. "Twenty thousand dollars. American." To him it's an excessive amount of money, and I'm thinking he blurted out such a number because there's a part of him that really doesn't want to go through with this. By asking for what he assumes to be an absurd amount he can dismiss me and save face. But the thing is, twenty thousand dollars is still much less than the sum I paid the girl to make sexual assault allegations against Bradley. "Done." I declare.

His eyes widen in surprise, no doubt it's more money than he makes in several years, even selling steroids. "Make that thirty."

"You're not doing this to me again." I shake my head and remain encouraged by the twinkle that's beginning to show in his dark, soulless eyes. "You'll get half now and the rest upon completion tomorrow." I can't afford this, which is why I'm lucky Rupert owes me that favour. At first, he'd been horrified by what I intended to do with the money but had been won over by my calm insistence it was necessary.

He stares at me hard and then laughs. "You white men really hate it when we niggers take your women."

I glance over at the coal burner but don't say he's welcome to her. "I need your bank details."

CHAPTER 7

Bushes

ARABELLA

This morning I dress in my very best yoga shorts, the purple ones that hitch almost up to my arse cheeks and which make those buns look impossibly pert and high, along with the top that displays my femininely sculpted abdominals and makes my breasts appear sumptuously attention grabbing.

All for a certain someone!

And if this doesn't work then I can't think what else, short of stripping down completely naked and forcing myself upon him, will, and I'm quite willing to go that far, I can assure you of that.

Sometimes I can see the temptation in his eyes, indeed, often it looks like all he wants to do is tear my clothes off my body himself but then it always seems like his stronger self gets the better of him, and then his mood changes, leaving me disappointed once more. I know the reasons, of course, because he's told me several times that he's engaged to his childhood sweetheart (really, how sweet is that, and the irony is this only makes me want him all the more) and you can trust me when I say that I hate the very thought of being one of *those* women, you know, the type who goes after men who're already taken, it's just that I see those arms, that bum, not to mention all the rest of him, and I just can't help myself.

And besides, Ashantay doesn't have to find out, right?

Sigh, but what I wouldn't give for a holiday fling with Kojo.

Just a fling, nothing more, and then I can return home to England, find a husband and nobody need ever know what went on over here.

Because what happens in Ghana, stays in Ghana, right?

I've grown accustomed to getting pestered by men wherever I go and it's just so cruel that the moment I find someone I want nothing more than to have mind-blowing sex with, over and over again, nothing I do seems to bloody work. Bloody hell, but what a time to lose my charms, right after meeting the hottest, friendliest, funniest, most interesting and sexiest man alive. Damn his muscles, Kojo's the total masculine package; biceps, triceps, deltoids, lats, traps, pecs, abs, and finally, those thighs and the way they bulge from beneath his baggy shorts and yes, you can bloody well bet that I've taken a sneaky look, several, in fact, at what else is lurking around that area. At first, I didn't think it was real, that maybe he keeps something strapped down there but then, after that orgasmic massage on the beach, I saw how it had moved even further down his leg, thickening to the point of impossibility. Just another inch or so and he'd have been poking indecently out the hem. Sigh.

And sigh again because the problem is, I tell myself for the fifty-thousandth time as I grab my coffee and head out for an early morning gym session, is that nothing seems to be working. Not the massage, not getting him to stand behind me barbell squatting as I push my bum into his waiting crotch, not crushing my breasts against him at every opportunity, not 'accidentally' grazing his substantial man-meat slow dancing the other night…

The other night…

What happened?

One moment he's staring down my blouse and the next he's receiving a phone call and dashing off without another word. I wanted so badly to ask what it was but yesterday he was absent from the gym, the beach too, which is odd, and now I have a terrible feeling that phone call was something truly bad.

Thinking once more about this, about him, I can't help but increase my pace because I can't wait to see him, to know that he's ok. He'll be there at the gym today, won't he? I can't wait to watch him sweating again, frustrating as I find it. Just a fling is all I desire, I say to myself again in the hopes that making it a morning affirmation will help make it come true. Two months of earth-shaking fireworks before I must leave this place and spend the rest of my life working and waking up beside the same man every single day for the rest of my life, whoever he might turn out to be. Is it really asking so much?

Feet scuff against gravel and then, out from nowhere, I find myself facing what might possibly be the largest, most muscular man in the entirety of West Africa. My first instinct is to appraise my safety because there's nobody else around, which then prompts me to question where in the bloody hell he just came from? Must have been from within the bushes that skirt the path. Weird.

I incline to my left to give him room to pass but he just stops altogether. Then steps to his right. Blocking my path. My heart beats faster. The gym is just up ahead. I incline to my right but he side-steps to his left. Blocking me again. This can't be real. I glance behind. Nobody else around. And now I'm close and he's still in the way.

"Um, excuse m…" I begin but find myself cut off when he lurches for me.

"Fuck! Yeah! White girl." His hands are sweaty and I manage to slip out from his grasp.

My heart leaps into my mouth and I don't know how, adrenaline, maybe, but the idea hits me immediately, and so I quickly unscrew the cap from my flask and chuck the coffee into his face.

"Aarrghhhh!!! Fucking bitch!"

I back away, my thoughts only of running, of screaming, but I can only make one step before his arms are back around me, this time my throat and mouth, and the next thing I know my heels are digging into the gravel, kicking up a cloud as I'm getting dragged back towards the bushes. The rustling of branches getting shoved aside fills my entire existence as several of them come swinging back to slash me across the face. I try so hard to scream, to wriggle free, but it's like my body has been overcome and deep down I know there's no way I could ever overpower such an enormous man.

"Stop squealing, bitch!" His voice, it's so deep, coarse, as he hauls me down to the ground and then the air is thrust out from my body as he dumps his considerable weight upon me, reaches down in front of himself and tugs down his shorts. He rips my yoga top, freeing my breast, and then attempts to manoeuvre so that he can tear away my shorts. All I want to do is transcend my body, or at the very least scream, but his hand is pressed down so hard against my mouth that I can barely even breathe.

I hear whistling coming from the path and someone stops by the opening where the bush has been damaged, but my eyes are too blurred to see much else, and I certainly can't scream for help. Mercifully, the man turns, sees, charges closer and leaps towards us, and then in a flash it's like my would-be rapist's entire weight is yanked away as he's pitched into an opening between two thorn bushes.

"Oww, fuck me!" Kojo? No! It's a familiar voice, one I most certainly know, and when I'm able to haul myself up I find Montgomery, Monty, is atop the beast raining down punches. "Nobody tries to rape a friend of mine, you brute."

That's right, Monty's started working out and now he's here, thank God.

My mouth plunges open, and I can see the blood on Monty, my saviour, the scratches caused by the thorns, the blood on his fists, and then he's pushed aside and the enormous man is pulling himself back to his feet before rushing away through the overgrowth.

CHAPTER 8

Steepled Hands

MONTGOMERY

I love it when a plan comes together.

She'd clung to me the entire drive to Aburi.

I wouldn't mind so much but the moment I stood and tried to leave the Humvee with both her hands still wrapped around my arm, I felt the leakage in my CKs at once, and now I'm pretty sure I've lost at least half the sack I was saving for our first time.

A first time that may now be coming sooner than I could ever have hoped.

"Are you sure you still want to go to work today?" Milly had asked, astonished, after the police officer had taken our statements and left.

Belle's breast had crushed even harder against my arm as her hold on me tightened, and it was the most wonderful feeling in the world. "I'm not about to let some awful attempted rapist defeat me." She'd blinked coyly in my direction and was so close that I could almost feel the breeze made by her eyelashes. "And besides, the safest place for me right now is with Monty." That she was calling me by the abbreviated version of my name was evidence enough something had changed.

"Wow!" Now even Milly was giving me a different kind of gaze, and if I didn't know any better…

"Mate," Rupert had pumped my hand for the fifth time, "judging from that guy's description, I'd say Belle's bloody lucky you just happened to be passing by after finishing your workout." Earlier, I'd told Rupert exactly what to say, words that would puff me up yet further while I'd let him, as I dismissed all praise like that guy who rescued those dozen kids from that flooded cave complex a while back.

"Just did what anyone else would do, is all." I'd flapped a dismissive hand, prompting gasps from both girls. Believe it or not, I was very nearly late at the rendezvous because three minutes earlier I happened to have been sticking a needle in my arse cheek.

"Bollocks, mate, *anyone* didn't happen to be just passing by though, did they, it was *you*." He'd shaken his head and looked at me all gooey-eyed. "And while I'd expect nothing less than for you to act so modest, there are times that your reluctance to accept all due praise and acclaim shocks even me."

"Well, you know…" I'd left it there as I flushed red and began to worry whether the imbecile was about to over egg the bloody pudding.

"I hate to break up this love fest," Milly had thankfully interrupted, "but our driver's here," she'd looked again with concern to Belle and then at me with a twinkle in her eye as she pushed out her chest, "and since everybody's safe and sound, all thanks to Monty, then I think we'd best get going."

Which brings us to now, and with Belle's unceasing proximity I can barely exit the vehicle with space enough to move my legs. Her trainers land on the dirt in pretty much the same time and space as my own, she's already facing me and I swear, but there's barely room to slip a credit card between my crotch and hers. The others laugh but Belle ignores them.

Her hand is in my hair. "You must let me take care of this graze." Her fingers run down my face to settle on the part of my cheek where the branch whipped into me. It hadn't been intended but now I think it's a nice little addition because a war wound makes the altercation even more authentic, and myself seem even more like a hero, a martyr, even.

I flinch. "It's nothing, babe, just a scratch."

She takes an involuntary gulp of air. "Don't you dare, Monty, one of the village women makes a special healing balm and I want to see this beautiful face restored, so that's enough of that silly talk, if you don't mind." Her fingers again brush over me and then our eyes meet no more than six inches apart, which is when it happens.

She presses her lips hard against mine and kisses me, and before I even know she's done it, she pulls away and is skipping in the direction of the community centre to catch up with the others, though not before glancing once back over a shoulder to give me the come here eye that can not be misinterpreted. It was a quick kiss, closed-mouthed, but easily the most exhilarating experience of my entire life and evidently, the rather embarrassing episode involving the steroids at the urinal is no longer an issue, because my pecker's throbbing so hard I fear it's about to explode. Most importantly, however, that kiss, the way it was done, everything about it was merely to whet my appetite. It was a promise of what's to come.

But this surreal morning only ratchets up a notch further because Belle glances to her left and then stops suddenly, only for a brief moment, before dashing the rest of the way to catch up with Milly and Rupert.

When I turn to look at the same spot I see Ingrid watching us from the threshold of old Mrs Tettay's shack.

IT'S NOT a day for work.

By eleven in the morning I've already been visited by so many people that there's barely any chance to dig the trench. And it's not merely my fellow do-gooders who come over to give me a pat on the back but I'm brought so many gifts by the villagers that eventually I have to start turning them down.

"You. Good man. Have this. Good man. You." It's an old woman who hands over what can only be described as a rattle on a long stick.

"Um, thanks, but you keep it."

"Take. Good man. Take."

Well, what else are you supposed to do other than graciously accept the gift? I wait for her to hobble off before slinging it in the ditch and covering it with earth.

"Jesus!" It's Jimmy spluttering the blaspheme when Ingrid makes her third visit of the morning out to see me. "I give up."

"Hello," she says in her sultry Scandinavian accent, leaning against a tree as she makes a show of overtly checking me out, all up and down-like. She's donned in blue medical scrubs because Marie's gone into labour, and it's telling that even under the circumstances she can't keep away from me. We flirt for a bit, talking about absolutely nothing of substance, and it's a wonderful feeling, as I stare at her pert boobs pushing out the blue garb that looks so sexy on her. A sophisticated woman. More so than any I've ever known. Belle and Milly included. *I wonder how Ingrid would feel about engaging in a threesome?* Unfortunately, however, I can't quite see Belle agreeing to such a thing so I force my perverted mind to drop the idea.

Thinking of a certain someone, Belle arrives, and that I didn't clap eyes on her approaching is very telling indeed. "You're wanted inside," she says to Ingrid in the sort of catty way girls can be with each other, it does not escape my attention.

"Excuse me," Ingrid says with exaggeration aimed at Belle before briefly softening her eyes to bid me farewell, for a few more minutes, I have no doubt. She then passes so close to Belle that they very nearly bump shoulders. I blow out air. Finally, that social proof phenomenon's working in my favour. Is this how life is for tall hunks carrying daddy's credit card? Fun for a while, no doubt, but I bet it gets tiresome eventually. Or maybe not.

Belle sidles up to me and I can just make out Jimmy swearing again from a short way up the excavation. She pulls out a small jar carved from wood. "The balm I promised." She doesn't even allow me to get a word in before she's jostling me back towards a tree stump where I'm forced to sit and then she's leaning over me, her enormous, plump breasts so close to my breathing apparatus that if I poked out my tongue I could lick her nipple, as she daubs my graze in a substance that stinks of baobab and matted monkey hair. When finished she gives her work one final touch with the tip of her finger and kisses me again on the lips, only this time it lasts for at least five full seconds, though still no tongue, however, she does not neglect to give my boner, which by now you can be sure is absolutely trembling, the slightest of brushes a second before sauntering back towards the main building.

I expel a blast of air as my head begins to spin. "Was that intentional?"

"Mate…" it's Rupert who calls over from the other side of the trench, and who you can be sure has been watching the whole spectacle. He says no more, because what else is there to say?

Together we twist towards raised voices coming from the visible part of the courtyard where they're just about to serve lunch. "What the fuck now?"

Because, no word of a lie, Belle and Ingrid are standing toe to toe as they yell at each other.

"I'm going to see how Jimmy's doing."

WORD IS that the baby's been born and now, long after lunch is finished, nearly all the volunteers are still waiting around for news from upstairs. Personally, I couldn't give less of a shit, though I'd much rather be sitting here next to Belle than straining my back out in the village, so I feign interest for that reason.

"If you ask me, she's the perfect feminine ideal," Jimmy, ever the trainee priest, is talking about Ingrid who right now is upstairs no doubt up to her elbows in piss, shit and blood, "brains, beauty, pedigree…"

"She's not a dog," Milly chips in.

"…money, and have you seen her in those feckin scrubs? They ought to outlaw those things." He shakes his head as I swear I can almost feel the irritation emanating from the object of my desires. "All I can say is … she'd best change into something plain and boring before tonight. A raincoat or even better, a tent ought to give her a moment's peace from the locals."

This is in reference to the fact that as soon as the day's toil is over, we're all catching a minibus for an evening out around the town in Accra. It's said to be a dual celebration of our arrival and the birth of Marie's child, though from what Jimmy says the group goes to Accra most Friday nights anyway because Winston performs his acoustic set in some jazz bar. Ever since we found out about this Rupert's been on the phone to a security company that boasts about providing muscle for some African big dick named Kwabena Duffuor. I know, don't ask.

"She's a bit bony, don't you think?" Belle remarks, all butter wouldn't melt.

"Exactly what I like, darling, exactly what I like."

"Well then, Jimmy, are you going to make a move on her tonight?"

"What?" He plucks at the crucifix dangling around his neck. "Have you forgotten about this?"

"So now you're acting all devout Catholic, are you?" Belle calls out across the table after allowing herself to get riled up by Jimmy's games, who's clearly enjoying himself. "Because you could have fooled me!"

Jimmy gives me the knowing eye. "Anyway, I reckon there's somebody else our perfect feminine ideal is interested in."

Belle's just about to scream at the man when the door opens and out steps Gabriel with his arm around his wife Marie who's holding a bundle wrapped in a swaddle. Everyone cranes their necks for a better look as the pair are immediately crowded and it's only when I stand that I see the way the tiny black face contrasts against the white of the cloth.

"Ugck, I've never been so disgusted to win a feckin bet," Jimmy declares to nobody in particular. "I think I'm going to be sick."

I know what he means, though the sentimental gooey sounds coming from both Milly and Belle confirms they don't share my views on certain subjects.

"And would you just look at the feckin cuck," Jimmy jerks his sunburned jaw to indicate Gabriel, "the way he's grinning like that. What is the feckin matter with him?"

Even though I share the sentiment, I can only shake my head in silence. I've spoken a couple of times with Gabriel, he's charming, funny and likeable, though the kicker is that he really does look like Henry Cavill of Superman fame, a fucking movie star, and that he would willingly throw his entire bloodline down the toilet is … is … well, I have absolutely no words for it. It's weird, strange and sick.

Cathy's first to kiss the baby and does so as she rubs her own paunch. "Say hello to your little half-brother," I just manage to hear from across the distance, her blurting out in the most dimwitted way imaginable what everybody's thinking but not daring to say, and right in front of the husband too.

Jimmy throws up his hands. "This whole feckin place is insane."

Ingrid is next to enter the courtyard and wipes her forehead as she approaches. "Well, that was an experience." She spots Belle, who's suddenly sliding almost on top of me, and there's definitely a small but noticeable jerking of the Swede's head when she notices. She takes a seat on my other side, prompting a stir from Belle. "Looks like you were right, Jim."

"I'm not happy about it," his mischievous eyes flick over Belle, "buuuut … now that Marie's gone and shat out a halfrican, I think you owe my friend Monty that hand job."

I feel Belle's entire body jump. I'd actually forgotten all about that, hard as it is to believe, what with everything else going on, and now there's only tension that follows with a long silence. But I can't keep this going, enjoyable as it is, not now, not when things are seriously heating up with Belle, no, I can't risk jeopardizing my future with her just for one quick release, incredible as I'm sure it would be. Perhaps if Belle hadn't been sitting next to me when Jimmy brought it up then I might have been tempted to suggest the two of us (that's Ingrid and myself) retire somewhere more private but right now that's not happening. Damn it. And damn Jimmy too.

We depart the courtyard and get back to work. Obviously, my mind remains on Ingrid wanking me off and so I resolve to hint she does just that very thing the next time she comes out for a visit, unfortunately, for the rest of the day the only time I see her is when she disappears yawning inside of old Mrs Tettay's mud hut.

Sitting at the back of the minibus while everyone piled in, I was waiting curiously for my first glimpse of this Winston enigma, alas, when the doors shut and we started grinding out the village in a cloud of sand I was prompted to ask whether or not we'd forgotten somebody who ought to be considered pivotal, bearing in mind he was performing the very acoustic set we were all going to watch. That was when Milly informed me he was already in Accra (how she came to know this information is another question entirely), getting ready for his set. Turns out Winston missed the birth of his biological son so that he could 'chill' with his homies.

"You give the man too much credit," Jimmy tells me, intentionally loud enough for Cathy, not to mention everybody else on the minibus to overhear. "He'll be smoking dope whilst balls deep in some groupie." He scratches at his arm and adds to the small pile of dead skin collecting at his feet. "What's one new son to him anyway? Seven months I've known this individual and I've lost count of the number of volunteers he's seduced and no doubt sent away pregnant, all because he's the guy in charge of that dust heap and can play a feckin guitar. I mean, it's not like you can just nip out to the pharmacy for a morning-after pill to exorcise the little turd from your body, is it? Natalia, Heather, Lauren, Georgia, Zoe and now Marie, I'll tell you this, he doesn't care about Marie's kid any more than he'll care about the next silly slut he knocks up."

Cathy twists around from the seat in front. "You small, bitter man." She reveals her phone and points the camera lens straight at Jimmy. "Just thought you'd like to know you'll be a

YouTube star by the end of the day." She twists back and a strained growling noise starts emanating from Jimmy's chest.

I take a breath as we enter the Accra suburbs. At the end of our first week in Aburi, I'm still not convinced this Winston guy really exists. Several times I've missed him in the community building, apparently, he coming down for lunch only after everybody else owing to his fasting schedule, or so I'm told, though you can be sure that not once has he bothered walking outside to see how his projects are coming along, and he certainly hasn't been concerned with introducing himself to me or Rupert. Oh, but he's introduced himself to the girls, though, you can be sure about that.

"We've chilled in his office." Belle had confirmed a couple of days ago when the subject was again brought up. "That's if you want to call it an *office*. In fact, I'd call it more of a residence, if anything. He showed us pictures of Jamaica and encouraged us to take a trip." *That* had made me squirm, might as well go for a holiday in HMP Belmarsh.

Rupert had blinked hard as he slowly turned toward his girlfriend. "Is this true?"

Milly had turned away and began occupying herself with her phone. "We've met," she'd said simply before changing the subject, "so what's on tonight then?"

Now, the minibus pulls up outside Bloom Bar and Rupert cranes his neck glancing out the window. "Thank God for that, they're here." This, I have no doubt, is in reference to our security. We begin stepping off the bus and Rupert's arm finds Milly's waist. "Darling, whatever you do, stay close to me at all times."

Her red eyebrows rise upon her forehead as the four of us land on the concrete to find ourselves enveloped by no fewer than nine large blacks in suits, ties, sunglasses and earpieces. Milly scowls at her boyfriend. "Bit over the top, don't you think?"

He shakes his head in a trembling sort of way. "Babes, this is Accra, don't be so bloody foolish."

"But everyone's looking at us, if anything, I'd say you're drawing more attention *to* us, you daft sod."

He makes a hushing sound in response and then the nine men are indicating that we should start for the club, which we do, and no sooner than entering does Milly shake her head before stepping outside the protective cordon and striding away, disappearing into the dimmed room that reeks of pungent sweat, weed and alcohol, and from where some jazz band is playing an instrumental.

"Milly!" Rupert yells, looking helplessly on at the security.

"Women," Jimmy adds helpfully from the outside, looking like a twelve-year-old who's been told he's not allowed to play with the big kids.

"You can't keep her away from the music, you know this." Belle, who appears to be finding this whole thing amusing, perks up, ever at my side. She peaks out through a gap between two of our detail and spots Ingrid shuffling inside the bar beside Greta, Kenny and Duncan, and smiles snidely in her direction.

It's not a large bar, I'd say more small and intimate, the perfect kind of place for an acoustic set. We're early but over the next couple of hours drinks and food are brought out as more people start to arrive and the atmosphere builds.

Belle feeds me a carrot, double-dipping it in hummus as her hip presses into mine. Earlier, she had our driver go back to the resort to fetch her red cocktail dress and it's the most impeccable thing I've seen in my entire life. The way it clings to her every curve, pushes out her sumptuous breasts and stops only a fraction of an inch below her arse cheeks ought to be illegal. "I'll see you soon," she kisses me on the lips and they part in lust as I can only stare at her walking away. Absolutely everything about Belle is perfection, ass, thighs, calves that pop in those heels. She knows what she's doing, no doubt about it, because what else am I expected to do but drool at her rear end as she struts away, as she's been stepping in and out of our cordon all night long, torturing me as intended. In fact, if I didn't know any better, I'd say that *she's* the one now trying to seduce *me,* which just goes to show how crazy things have become. Giving me a coy glance from across the dance floor, Belle arrives beside Milly, who's looking so entranced by the music she might have been one of Charles Manson's cult members. Not for the first time tonight Ingrid takes Belle's temporary absence as an invitation to approach.

She slinks up, her arse brushing against my boner in a way that cannot have been accidental. "So … Marie's baby was born black…"

The unwelcome reminder causes my belly to lurch in that now familiar yet uncomfortable way. "Aye."

She leans closer. "So…"

It takes a moment for me to realize what she's hinting at. "Oh! Um, you mean the hand…" her buttocks again brush my quivering phallus. You know, I'm seriously fucking tempted but I also want to remain resolute, to save myself for Belle, because I'm beginning to hope that tonight might just be the night. One might say I'm conflicted in the most wonderful way imaginable.

Ingrid's lips meet my ear. "Perhaps we can get a hotel," her breath causes a delightful shiver to orgasm down my spine, "and maybe I'll give you more than just a hand job."

Mercifully, I think, I'm spared having to disappoint the girl when Rupert leans in between us. "Ingrid, you wouldn't mind if I have a word in private with Monty, would you?"

She scowls at him. "What, right now?"

His unsettling grimace answers for him and she shuffles away to go speak with Duncan and Greta. Rupert jerks his bearded jaw towards Milly who right now is looking worryingly reminiscent of a sixties hippy chick at Woodstock.

"She's intentionally revealing her wild streak tonight, Monty, why won't the bloody girl come back inside here with us where it's safe?"

To be honest, I'm beginning to wonder if hiring nine large blacks was a bit overkill, and several times I've seen two or three of them giving us odd glances. But I definitely detect my friend's exasperation and almost fear asking, "how's the plan going, big guy?"

Monday night he was too drunk, Tuesday they had that argument, Wednesday they were both too tired after work and last night he told me he had a bad dose of food poisoning after trying the grilled tilapia at one of the resort restaurants. His face clams up. "Tonight's my last chance, Monty, so it looks like it's now or never." Not strictly true because Milly won't depart for the dance troupe until the new year, which leaves at least one more egg after this one, ready and waiting to be fertilized, though knowing my friend as I do, he'll only find several more ways of squandering that one as well, each and every night. No, tonight is pretty much it for Rupert and Milly, sad as I am to admit it.

I can only think about yesterday when he was up all night splattering the en suite toilet bowl. "Are you sure you're feeling up to it?"

"Whether I'm feeling up to it or not is beside the point," he says slamming his drink down. At least he gets it now, finally. And neither can he take his eyes from Milly, who right now is looking ravishing in a flowing white dress with a long slit that displays her sculpted rower's legs almost to the snatch. Naturally, there's a crowd of large, confident, black-skinned locals surrounding her and if I didn't know any better I'd say she definitely appears to be delighting in the attention. A tear rolls down Rupert's cheek. "I can't lose her, Monty, I just can't. It will be the death of me."

My mouth parts, I'm not good with this sort of thing, having to deal with fully grown men crying in a crowded bar on a Friday night when I'm expecting to get laid myself tonight. I'm just about to demand he pulls himself together when the bar lights dim, the walk-in music turns off and the stage spotlights switch on.

And then what has to be Winston begins lightly strumming from the stage.

A loud cheer rolls over from the front as I can only squint in that direction. I'm looking at a slender negro with his legs stretched out in front, crossed at the ankles, as he leans idly back in a La-Z-Boy, his guitar perched on his lap as he plucks away at the strings. He's got shoulder-length dreadlocks left free to roam and enough lines and experience in his facial features for me to place him in his mid-thirties. While definitely not one of those typical ugly-as-fuck blacks, he's certainly not in Kojo's league when it comes to facial aesthetics, as hard as it is for me to admit. When he starts to sing his voice is almost as deep as Barry White's, and damned if I can understand a bloody word of it.

When the first song finishes three large negresses rush the stage for an embrace. Winston barely troubles himself to swat them off, not that he could even if he tried. Finally, it takes security to remove the women from when he's finally able to start the second song, another slow one that I can't understand in the slightest, though after a couple of minutes I'm surprised to find my foot tapping to the rhythm regardless.

There's something to be said for magnetism, or maybe there isn't, because I'm thinking it's one of those things that's hard to define or describe. Obama has it, supposedly, and JFK was known to have it in abundance. Going further back there were many great leaders who had it; Caesar, Napoleon, Mustache Man; that certain indescribable something that makes men follow them and women spread their legs willingly for them. I can't say for sure whether Winston has it from what little I've seen. What I can say is that he does possess a certain unspoken something, charisma perhaps. Or maybe it's just the fact that he's actually a pretty damned good musician.

The second song finishes and there's another rush of women onto the stage. From my side, there's what can only be described as a horrified whimper and it takes a second to realize it came from Rupert. It's only when I twist back to face the front that I find Milly's one of the women who's stormed the stage, one of about six who's now jostling to get closer to Winston and in doing so, she unceremoniously shoves aside a black woman almost twice her size. Winston tips back his head to laugh before doing nothing as Rupert's entranced girlfriend throws her arms around his neck as she plants rapid kisses on his cheeks and lips.

"Why won't they drag her off?" Rupert truly says as though it's everybody else's fault that his girlfriend's publicly losing her mind. Finally, it's one of Milly's dark-skinned rivals who wrests off her fingers before flinging her halfway across the floor.

There's an intermission and I take the opportunity brought by a return to the walk-in music to give my friend a much needed pep talk. "Ok, listen, you have got to do it tonight, do you understand me?"

His jaw sets strongly as he regards me with strong eye contact. Good. "Yes," he states matter of fact with a resolute voice.

My hands are on his shoulders and I'm giving him a shake. "Ignore what you've just seen. She's acting this way because, clearly, she's ovulating. Her body's screaming at her to get pregnant, which is why she's throwing her snatch at whoever the fuck she perceives to be the nearest alpha male, you got that? If she'd been watching the set from back here then it would've been your dick she'd be throwing herself upon, right? So tonight, my friend, you need to make sure it's your dick she lands on. Tonight, the moment we get back to the chalet, you need to lock her in that room and don't even think about leaving until you've emptied a sackful inside of her. Do you understand me?"

He rolls up his sleeves and thrusts out his chest. "Yes!"

I slap him hard on the chest. "Then go get her! Tell her we're leaving in ten minutes."

And then, with the look of a child taking his first steps on two feet, he glances once to his left at the large men in dark suits watching over him, and then again to his right before confidently striding, alone, out from our protective cordon.

I can only shake my head as I feel my own tears beginning to well. Luckily, I manage to bite them back because Belle's back at my side.

She squashes her tits against my chest. "Did I just hear you say we're leaving?"

CHAPTER 9
Pinnacle

MONTGOMERY

"Do you think Ingrid's pretty?" Belle breaks off from crushing her lips against mine for long enough to hiss into my ear. Right now, she's feeling incredibly insecure and I absolutely love it.

"Nuh-uh," I tug her by the hair and her lips are soon back where they belong, where they've always belonged, and the caresses of her tongue against mine is the greatest feeling in the world. I'm barely even aware that our limousine is cruising through traffic, my head is that high up in the clouds, and it can't be long before I'm back at the resort and in Belle's bed, my dream finally being realized.

She hums delightfully into my mouth, her hand rubbing the spot just above my knee, though admittedly an unwelcome distance from my throbbing cock, the way things are going I'm sure she'll arrive there in due course.

My hand ever on Belle's tit, I give her another squeeze, not giving a fuck that Rupert and Milly are almost certainly taking peeks from the other side of the glass partition. Right now there's absolutely nothing in the whole fucking world I care more about than continuing to squeeze Belle's tit with my hungry hand. From memory, she's far larger than that escort I paid a fortune to fuck in Istanbul though, remarkably, she's probably about the same size as Miss Happy Cakes, despite being half the bodyweight, and Belle's breasts are infinitely firmer. Most of all, however, it's Belle! I'm feeling the breasts of the girl I've been infatuated with for five whole fucking years.

She croaks against me, "what are you going to do to me when we get back?"

I almost choke on my own saliva that's rapidly filling my mouth. Fuck, what am I *not* going to do to her!? "I … I'm going to cum in all your fucking holes," which is true, though admittedly I probably should have given my words a second's thought before blurting out the first obscene thing that popped into my head, mind, it's not that I can help myself, not when right now I'm being controlled entirely by Little Monty.

She shuffles in a way that causes her arse cheek to squeak against the leather upholstery. "Let's … maybe start with something a little more regular, don't you think?" There's the slightest, yet noticeable, twitching of that area of skin between her eyes.

I suck in air. "Yes, yes, of course, sorry-sorry."

She takes my hand and moves it onto her buttock. "Don't forget the rest of me, I'm perfect all over."

I swear there's a miniature ejaculation inside my underwear. "Right!" My hand trembles as my fingers sink into her flesh, the hard musculature of an athlete's buttocks. If we're not home soon then I can't guarantee I won't get carried away in the backseat of our ride. "Fuck, how much further?" I blink away the fog to find we're entering the resort, finally, which is when I make eye contact with Rupert through the glass. I get the awful impression he's been watching me and Belle this whole time, while Milly's body's turned away as she stares absently outside.

She hadn't been happy about being dragged away before

the end of Winston's set and the rest of us had watched her discontented gesticulations from the doors.

"Serves her right for making a public spectacle of herself, and right under Rupert's nose too." Jimmy had shaken his head in disgust. "Tell him he'd best keep her on a tight rein from now on. We don't want another Natalia on our hands."

I'd squinted at him. "Natalia?" Obviously another story he was dying to tell me.

"Aye, Natalia, Russian, and yet another blonde, obviously. She was the daughter of one of those oligarchs you hear about, and the most striking girl you ever saw, even more so than Ingrid, with legs all the way up to her arse. Apparently, she was one of the top ballet dancers in Moscow too, which explained it." He'd made a strange circular motion with his hips and I'd stupidly glanced down to find a small lump protruding from his jeans. "Anyway," he'd flapped a hand toward the stage, "it all started in this very bar. She was just some tourist no doubt trying to 'find herself,'" he'd said with a mocking tone, "and after seeing *him*," he invested the word with hatred, no doubt referring to Winston, "well, what do you know, but the very next day she just happened to turn up in Aburi."

I could already see where this was going and pinched at the skin atop my nose. "And?"

"Do you really need to ask?" His jaw had clenched. "After a couple of weeks she had to dash off back to Russia, no doubt so that she could plausibly pass the pregnancy off as the boyfriend's she supposedly had. What she thought she'd do after giving birth is beyond me but then, as we know, the fairer sex isn't exactly known for thinking that far ahead, are they?" He did that weird gyrating thing with his hips again. "You can find her now on OnlyFans, abandoned by her boyfriend, father and everyone else, a single mum living off donations as she shows off her little niglet to the world."

I'd sighed. "How is that even remotely the same as Rupert and Milly?"

He'd shrugged. "Ok, maybe it's not, but you don't want it to end up being *even remotely the same*, do you, which is why I'm telling you. I don't know what it is about him, the guitar, his so-called aura, his stupid feckin dreadlocks, I don't know, but women, for whatever reason, go bat shit feckin loopy for that big-lipped Rastafarian."

Now, I begin to panic on Rupert's behalf and fire off a quick text, imploring him to slide closer to Milly, to start making her feel good, her pussy moist, and best of luck with it. His section of the limo lights up and he glances down into his screen. He nods and after a second he slides across the seat and places an arm around her, and I don't know how he manages it, Shakespearian sonnets whispered into Milly's ear or something, but by the time we're exiting the limo and strolling for the chalet, their body language is similar to that of mine and Belle's, their arms around each other as they stop every few steps for another smooch.

Because I was about to have sex with the love of my life.

I'M FUMBLING with the key, my hand shaking as I plunge it into the hole and twist.

"Come on, Monty, let us in!" It's Milly who surprises me by being in a rush to get to bed but then, I remember, if she's truly ovulating then it makes sense and would also explain her sudden eagerness to get my buddy's dick inside of her. What a wonderful evening this is about to become; Rupert might very well conceive and I'm about to make love with Belle.

"Yes, be quick!" My girl agrees, and a second later we're all piling in through the opened door, and we're all so impatient to take things to our respective rooms that we don't even bother turning on the lights.

My lips are on Belle's as we sidestep towards the bedroom that I have no doubt we'll soon be sharing, there's a bump and an "ouch" as Rupert clatters into the countertop and then Milly's calling across the room to declare, "goodnight!"

I don't even bother answering, I'm literally quivering with anticipation, still quite unable to believe this is truly about to happen. Belle opens the door to her room with her bum as we edge back over the threshold. I feel hastily across the wall for the light switch because there's no way I want anything less than perfect vision for *this*, to experience her body to the full. Will she look as good as I've always fantasized? Of course, she will! I find the switch and when the lights flick on Belle's still there, truly, right before me, and no less possessing an expression that tells me she actually wants this herself. Life can be funny sometimes, and truly wonderful.

She moves towards the curtains, pulls them closed, and then turns around so that I'm staring straight at the curvature of her arse. I feel a twitch immediately. She begins edging back, I don't move, and neither does she stop until her buttocks meet my raging stiffy. She wiggles her shoulders. "My zip."

I make an odd groaning sound as my fingers meet her back and I waste no time tugging down the zip and exposing the flawlessly clear flesh of her back. She kicks off her heels, dropping in height so that now I'm a tiny bit taller than she is, which bestows upon me some extra confidence I'm in need of right now because my entire body's shaking. She wiggles out from the straps and allows the dress to collapse to the ground, and by this point you can be sure my dick's throbbing so badly that it's actually quite painful.

"Unclip my bra," she commands, and I do what she says at once, in my haste accidentally breaking the cheap plastic clasp. Best keep quiet about that.

And then she turns around.

"Oh, fuck me!" I take an involuntary step back just so that I can appreciate her, the remarkable plump fullness of her breasts, their perfect round symmetry and size. My hands are on them at once, seizing, feasting, squelching them.

"Hey," her hands are on my wrists, "go easy there, Monty."

"Oh, yes, sorry, of course," that odd groaning sound emanates from inside of me again but if she notices then she's too kind to say anything about it, "I'll be gentler from now on."

She nods and thrusts her breasts forwards again. "So, you like what you see?" What a ridiculous fucking question. Am I supposed to come up with something witty in the heat of the fucking moment when all that's racing through my head is getting my dick inside of her as quickly as fucking possible?

I ignore it and instead wrap my mouth around her nipple, giving it a swirl with my tongue whilst tugging her closer by the arse so that the entire boob squashes against my face. I couldn't get anymore of her inside of me if I tried, which I do regardless, whilst at the same time attempting to tug down her red lace underwear. I'm so overcome by her taste that I'm slow to react to the reality that her snatch is now exposed, if only I'd just glance down and take a gander.

She flinches. "Ok, I think we're done with that." When she backs away her nipple's red raw, there are teeth marks just above her delightfully reddening areola and no small quantity of saliva reflecting the light from above.

"Sorry-sorry, I, ugh, sorry…"

"It's ok, here," she reaches up and behind, pulls out the bobble and then there's a giant tumble of blonde that unleashes a wave of lavender over me, "you like?"

If I was getting carried away before, I'm not sure how the fuck I'm supposed to take *this*. "Um," I swallow, "maybe we should just fuck now."

She squints. "Oooor, we could, maybe, build up to that. But go gentle, alright?"

I nod, "uh-huh." I stagger forward and pull her towards me again, our lips connecting, dancing, engaging in their own little love making session. She tastes so wonderful, like the finest of wines, as her scent plays the devil in my head. I move a hand from her arse around to her front, immediately finding her folds and then, Jesus fucking Christ, I'm literally touching Belle's slit, rubbing around the moisture and slipping a finger inside.

She pants against me and presses herself harder against my digit, but, knowing the size of my cock, I'm definitely wary about allowing her to sink too far down, after all, I'd like her to know I'm there for the main event. I retract a little but she only follows up by sinking down again.

She reaches for my hand and pants, "please, another … another finger."

Fuck that! But what am I supposed to do, say no? And I'm still fully fucking dressed here. "You know, it's getting hot, let me just…" I tug off my sweater and begin working on my first shirt button when she turns around and positions herself on the bed, her arse poking in the air as her juicy cunt is presented right to me. I skip the shirt and go straight for my zipper.

"Maybe start by tasting me?" She says with such sultry confidence that I'm already at her buttocks, lowering down to my knees and moving forwards with my face. My tongue's an inch away from her slit when there's an almighty scream from the next room.

"Oh, what was that?" She twists around causing my snout to slap against her arse.

"Nothing," I grab ahold of her hips and attempt to steer her back in situ, "I didn't hear anything, you're imagining things."

"No, I definitely…"

"Quiet!" I snap. "And stay fucking still." I forge on again, only to be interrupted by the opening and slamming of the door belonging to the bedroom of the obvious two people.

"Belle!" It's Milly's upset shouty voice.

"Fucking bastard!" I snarl. "Can't he for once…"

In an instant, Belle's back on her feet wrapping a throw around her golden shoulders and heading for the door. I stand and feel the ooze that's dribbled all the way down my leg, grab a handful of hair, tug, and follow after her.

When I arrive in the main room the girls are hugging, the throw not quite covering Belle's arse, while Milly's dressed in a gown and has tears streaming down her face. Belle brings her to arms length. "Babe, what's up?"

"He … he…" Milly palpitates, "he tried to have … he tried to stick it in me unwrapped." Belle gasps, her jaw dropping just as the door inches open and Rupert steps sheepishly out.

"Fuck!" I cringe, covering my eyes. "Mate, would you put some bloody clothes on."

Belle sees the obvious and lets out an involuntary mocking laugh. Rupert places his hands over himself and continues plodding out.

There's a terrible persisting silence as I'm getting an awful feeling he's fucked up somehow, despite all my best efforts at giving him advice. Wait! Hang on. What did Milly just say? Oh fuck! He *has* fucked up!

Finally, Belle throws up her palms. "What … what did you just try to do? Is … is this true, Rupert?"

His expression says it all, that he indeed attempted to stealth his bird. Rupert's gaze leaves the ground only for long enough to look briefly up at me. "It was Monty's idea." Fuck! There it is.

Both girls give me identical prolonged angry looks as my mouth attempts to find the words. But what can I even say? Clearly, Rupert ain't man enough to take responsibility for his own sex life.

"Thanks, mate," I tell him, confirming to both girls that it was indeed my idea for Rupert to stealth Milly, which it was, I know, but did my best mate have to grass me the fuck up? Oh, I could have denied it, quite easily in fact, but the one tiny, minute, minuscule detail is that Rupert happens to have just a little bit of dirt on me, namely the purchasing of attempted rapey services from a certain large gym brute. No, far better I hold my hands up and admit my part in this, relatively, minor incident by comparison in the hopes my dimwitted friend doesn't land me in the shit any further. No, it's far better to defuse the situation here, take the loss now and hope to say all the right words to Belle later, which would be far preferential to a heated exchange between four horny individuals where certain incriminating things might easily be said in the heat of the moment.

I touch a hand to my heart. "I just wanted my best friend to be happy."

"By doing *that*?" Milly screeches. "I shouldn't have to tell you that's how pregnancies happen and you," she whips around on her boyfriend, "you know I'm departing for the London Festival Opera! Are you trying to destroy my entire future?"

Again, the imbecile's expression gives up the game entirely.

Both girls emit crazy exasperated sounds. "You … you *are* trying to prevent me from going, from … from leaving you, aren't you?" Milly hisses.

Rupert again looks up from the floor to make brief eye contact with me. "Monty said it was the only way." Both girls whip around again on me.

And yet again, for the same reasons, I have to take this, and so I bow my head in turn. "Yes, this is correct, I did." My candidness actually shocks them.

"Are you proud of yourself?" Belle asks quite reasonably. There's no answer to that but luckily Milly interjects.

"So, Monty, you gave him the idea to get me pregnant in order to stop me from working, is that what you did?"

"Yes," I confirm simply, my hands clenching into tight fists as I bite back the urge to go on the defensive, to pass some of the blame onto Rupert, because obviously I can't risk things escalating while he's standing there. No, I'll just have to wait until I'm back alone with Belle to plead my case.

After another prolonged silence, Milly finally says to Rupert. "You're sleeping on the couch." She dashes back into their room before returning with a blanket and throwing it at him.

I exhale, drape my arm across Belle's shoulders and gesture with my jaw towards our bedroom. "Come on, let's go."

She steps quickly away, though when she turns around her face appears conflicted over what to do. "I … I think I'd best spend the night with Milly tonight. She's pretty upset." She rubs my arm, which is a great fucking relief considering everything, and I'm convinced that despite tonight's revelations things are not destroyed with Belle. Oh, don't get me wrong, I've got arguably the worst case of blue balls in the history of mankind, but I'll gladly take that if by tomorrow we can get back on track with the sex.

"You're right," I nod before giving her a peck on the cheek and turning around for her bedroom.

"Um," she begins, grabbing me by the hand and smiling, "you wouldn't mind the couch tonight, would you?"

I almost argue about it, given it's an empty fucking bed that'll go wasted, but under the circumstances I decide not to argue the toss. "That's fine."

So, tonight, I fall asleep on the couch along with a fully naked Rupert.

CHAPTER 10

A Double Case Of Epididymal Hypertension

MONTGOMERY

R upert and I only rouse when both girls return from the gym, the pair of them wearing stretchy workout garb that instantly reminds me I've got a bad case of blue balls, while doubtless Rupert's undergoing a similar feeling.

Milly blends protein shakes as Belle pours porridge into two bowls and it's only now that I've had a minute for my brain to start working that an awful panicking sensation floods my body.

What if they'd seen Milky at the gym?

I spring up from the couch. "Everything alright?"

Belle squints at me. "Um, yes, how about you?"

I slowly exhale. I hadn't even thought about the possibility of Belle and her attempted struggle snuggler crossing paths again but the fact he wasn't there most likely means he's been arrested, and good riddance. Perhaps, at the very least, he's decided to lay low for a while which, you never know, might ultimately mean I won't have to pay him the rest of the money. "Just worried about your safety, is all, darling."

"I've got my girl here." She squeezes Milly's arm, which only makes me feel disappointed. Is she saying she doesn't need *my* protection anymore? "After all," she continues, "you can't be everywhere, and the two of you looked so peaceful sleeping together." She sniggers, it sounds encouraging enough, though it's also a bit of a put-down. Milly, I note, has a face like an Easter Island stone statue, and refuses to even look in our direction. Rupert's awake, I can tell, though is pretending not to be.

"Right." I scratch my head and say to Belle, "um, I was wondering if you wanted to come for a walk along the beach with me?"

"Awe, that sounds nice, but Milly and I have already decided to head into Accra."

"Accra?" This doesn't sound good at all. "Don't you think that's a little dangerous?"

She shakes her head. "No need to worry about our safety. Winston says he's going to show us around a few spots with some friends of his."

"Ok." It's a great effort not to react to this appalling piece of news and I feel a foreboding angst begin churning around in my belly.

She approaches from the kitchen, leans close and speaks softly into my ear. "Maybe we can have dinner together. Tonight. I think there are some things we need to discuss." It's a fucking crisis dinner.

I swallow. This could be good or bad.

And there's nothing I can do but nod.

IT'S THE LONGEST, most awful day of my life.

I try to remain occupied, though there's only so much time you can spend lifting weights at the gym before exhausting yourself. I head for the toilets and inject my buttock with another dose of Testosterone Cypionate, remembering too late it was only yesterday I'd last taken the drug. I walk along the beach on my own, thinking only of Belle, what she's doing and who she's doing it with, and am so preoccupied by morbid thoughts that I can't even bring myself to eat lunch.

Time drags.

I see Rupert doddering along in the surf, no doubt going through his own personal torment, but I turn around in order to avoid him. Right now, I can do without having to deal with his shit as well as my own.

"What the fuck happened?" I'd asked him last night, for the fifth time batting his foot away from my face.

He'd sniffed. "She saw in the mirror, Monty."

It's not until seven in the evening that I receive a text from Belle that reads, 'meet you in the bar in one hour.'

I'm cautiously hopeful. If she wants nothing more to do with me then she'd have said so, surely. At least that's what I tell myself.

I'm early to the bar and now sit alone with two beers, fidgeting and looking up at every new face that enters. When it's ten minutes after the rendezvous time I consider firing her a message to ask where she is, but decide against it. At half an hour I'm seriously beginning to get worried. It's not until forty-five minutes later when she strolls into the bar and I immediately notice something different about her.

She takes the seat on the opposite side of the booth, not beside me, as my eyes fix on the single braid that at some point during the day has been weaved into her angelic blonde hair, almost like she's beginning some sort of transition, but to what? It even has a bead dangling at the end like you see with so many African women.

"Thanks," she gestures to the beer, "but I think I've already had enough for one day."

"Oh…"

"But you go ahead," she prods the full glass closer to me and leans back, and never did she feel so distant, or look so beautiful. It actually hurts, so much so that I'm temporarily speechless.

"How was your day?" I'm nervous about asking, just in case, you know, my worst fears…

The smile lights up her face. "It was wonderful. You and Rupert really should get out and explore more."

"Me and Rupert, right…"

"The food is amazing, oh, and the museums, the Old Town, markets, people. It's a wonderful country." She's so perfect in this flowery dress she's wearing, the way her cleavage wants to spill out over the top, and I can't stand the thought of her having been seen, stared at, watched, propositioned even, by so many African men today. "Milly wanted to stay out longer," she continues, "so she's gone to a bar with Winston and…"

"Winston?" I interject.

"If you let me finish…" she shakes her head, "with Winston and a bunch of the others from Aburi."

"Cathy?"

Her head snaps back. "How did you know that?" Oh shit!

"Just a guess." I can't stand it any longer and have to get it all off my chest now. "Belle, what's happening between the two of us?"

She reaches across the table to grab my hand and my heart sinks as I prepare for the worst news of my entire life. "You really impressed me yesterday … um, not just about that terrible incident in the morning, the other thing, when Rupert was caught … the way you immediately came clean about the part you played in it." She squeezes my hand as her words, not to mention her tone of voice, actually offers encouragement. "I mean, don't get me wrong, it was a ratty thing to do but…" her smile slowly grows, "if I'd had any doubts about you before last night, there are none now. I mean, irrespective of the problems Milly and Rupert might be going through right now, I don't see why any of that should affect us. I … I think I can trust you." She smiles seductively. "And you'll always be the guy who saved me from getting raped and possibly worse."

I take an enjoyable slow exhalation of lavender infused air, grab her hand and guide her around to my side of the booth, telling her to sit, and the intensification of the lavender scent makes my boner throb so badly it's painful. I cup her cheeks in my hands and lean forwards for the kiss, and if there was any doubt remaining that she wanted this, that she wanted *me*, then there can be no misinterpreting the enthusiasm of her tongue as it clashes with mine.

I pull away, food the last thing on my mind even though I've barely eaten all day. "You're not hungry are you?"

"Not at all."

"Shall we get out of here?"

"Yup!" She squeezes my hand but as we both move to slide out from the booth there's a woman stomping across the bar in our direction.

"Oh, fuck!" I mutter under my breath because I recognize the slut, and I'm already glancing left, right and behind for another door or failing that a spare table to crawl beneath but there's nothing, and neither is there any more time.

"You absolute prick!" Milky's ho bites.

Belle, still confined in the booth, twists around to stare wide-eyed in my direction. "Monty?"

"Ignore her," I can't move out for Belle so I give her buttocks a push but she can't move either because now she's being physically blocked by the woman with the large booty.

The madwoman places both hands down on the table and leans down, exposing two mountains of cleavage. "Yes, that's right, try to escape, you little shit."

Belle grabs her hand and tries to remove it from the table but nothing's shifting, not even an inch. "What's the matter with you? Let us go, you…" she pauses while something in her brain starts to grind. "I know you, don't I?"

The ho's lip curls upwards. "We've met, briefly, I'm sure."

Belle shoots me another look, her eyebrows dipping in confusion before twisting back. "Well, what do you want?"

"Nothing," I interject while trying to stand but the booth's confines are so tight there's no way to even straighten my legs. No, the cunt has us both trapped and you can bet I'm not so naive as to be clueless as to where this might possibly lead.

"This prick," why does she keep calling me that? "is responsible for Osei being arrested and for us getting kicked off the resort."

I find my voice. "I know of no man by the name Osei and neither do you appear to have been 'kicked off the resort,' you daft moose, now, I've had just about enough of..."

She slams her phone down to the table, the screen filled with Milky's terrifyingly brutish image as he takes a selfie in the mirror, his bottom half wrapped in a towel as every vein pops from his monumental chest as he flexes.

Belle gasps and instinctively scans her surroundings for an escape, panicking. "That's him, that's him! How...how do you..."

"He's my man!" She actually says with pride. "And he would never do what you've accused him of."

Belle's turned white. "How...how could you date such a..."

"I told you," she snaps, "Osei would never do such a thing."

"Ignore her words, my sweet, she's clearly insane, this man's a monster, you know this." I again try to shove Belle out the booth but one angry glare from the mudshark is enough to prompt us both to remain in our seats.

"You absolute prick," the slut directs at me, "are you sure there's nothing you'd like to confess?"

"Confess?" Belle switches between the two of us while all I want to happen is for the ceiling to come falling in. African building codes are hardly known to stand up to Western standards and yet here we are, sitting beneath tonnes of watered-down concrete and absolutely nothing bad is happening. Why are we not, even now, getting crushed beneath an avalanche of debris, it's most outrageous.

"I … I don't know what she's talking about," I'm glancing manically about for security, "can someone please help? Help! Help!"

The coal burner slides a finger across the screen. "Go on," she says to Belle, "press play."

Belle's shaking her head and for a moment I even believe she's not about to tap the screen, but then she does, and she gasps immediately. "Monty, what's this?"

I cover my eyes, unable to watch, and yet neither can I look away. It's a video of the woman performing a heavy barbell squat, working that booty, while in the background I can clearly be seen chatting casually with Belle's attempted rapist.

"In a moment you'll see him buying anabolic steroids," she adds helpfully, which is about the least of my sins about to be exposed by this rancid cunt.

Belle whips around on me. "You…Monty…you know this man?"

I squint at the screen. "Is it the same person, kinda hard to tell, don't you think?"

"It looks like the same person to me," Belle insists with rising anxiety in her voice. Ok, sure, but what does this video even prove? That someone I once had a conversation with tried to rape her. I'd still have come to her rescue and saved the day regardless.

The bitch slides her finger across the screen, bringing up the next video. "Note the timestamp. This is the very next morning, a day before you *met* my man." Oh, fuck!

This next video also shows us talking while she squats in the foreground and there's a worrying lack of gym music, in fact, I'd say, you can almost hear some of what we're saying, words like, "tomorrow morning," "bushes," "$20,000," and finally, "rescue." If all that wasn't incriminating enough, I'm there, plain as day slowly swiping at the air with my fists in what could only be described as some kind of mock rehearsal. This bitch had given me a bad feeling right from the off. What did I tell you? Instincts! And despite being honed, what good have they done for me?

Belle's hand, which throughout the altercation has remained stoically holding onto mine, now wilts away. She turns away from me and speaks directly to the horrible woman. "What, um, what was that about $20,000, erm, and bushes, and…"

The woman snatches up her phone and stuffs it down her cleavage. "This creature that you're sitting with paid Osei $20,000 to," her rancid face clamps up as she struggles to say the words, "*do* what he did to you so that this one, Rupert, I believe, could come to the rescue and save the day, no doubt so that he could get into your pants." She snorts with contempt like the pig that she is. "And from the looks of it, his plan worked."

Belle instinctively slides away from me. "His plan did *not* work!" She shakes her head suddenly. "I'm sorry, you said *Rupert*?"

The witch nods. "Rupert, yes, the name of the bank account the money came from." I can only sigh into my hands as Belle twists around so that she can thump me on the shoulder.

"And you got your best friend involved in this too?" An involuntary yelp emits from her. "I bet Milly will be interested to hear about this." Well, I suppose that would be karma for grassing me up for the whole stealthing idea so I won't intervene there, especially not if it means some of this shit can be deflected from me, not that by this point it'll make any difference. Milly thumps me again. "Have you got nothing to say for yourself?" I remain slumped. "No, on second thoughts, don't say anything, I don't ever want to hear another word from you ever again."

I'd cry if I could. But there reaches a point when things become so bad and so hopeless that you've passed the point where crying is even possible. No, instead I feel only a combination of numbness, regret, hurt, rage, loss, anger and an overwhelming urge for vengeance.

Belle places her hand on top of this woman's. "I don't know what to say. As you know, I had nothing to do with any of this. I just hope that you and Osei come through this unscathed. If you need me to speak to the police about anything, to retract my statement, or whatever, then here's my number." She writes it down on a napkin and hands it over.

"Thank you," the ogress says for the first time with a measured voice, "and best of luck yourself. Maybe go back to that sweet local man I saw you with at dinner the other day, you deserve happiness too." And then, having wrecked my entire life, the vicious, nasty fucking cunt is striding away, taking that monumental booty with her.

I cower beneath my hands for a little longer and soak up the darkness. I'd better get used to this feeling. It's only now that I realize my balls have shrivelled up so much that it's alarming, though probably understandable considering the circumstances. Beside me, Belle remains. I feel her shaking. I … I don't think this is repairable. "Fuck!" I groan and reason that even if the ceiling did fall in, being buried alive beneath a thousand tonnes of rubble couldn't possibly be any worse than this. In fact, I don't think tonight could possibly get any worse.

"Hello, Monty, my friend."

The first to react is Belle, obviously, doing so with a feminine shriek of delight as she almost falls over herself to escape this booth before leaping immediately into the arms of Kojo.

He now catches her in those strong arms, the impossibly

tight t-shirt he's wearing revealing the impressive peaks from his biceps as they easily take her weight. Not one of us has so much as heard from Kojo since three nights ago, and the truth is I was beginning to hope we'd seen the last of him. Not so. And now, despite the fact his face is being smothered in kisses, it's *me* he's staring at, cold and hard.

Finally, Belle pulls away. "Kojo? Where have you been? Oh, what's wrong?"

He places her down and I don't know if Belle can see it but to me, he doesn't look like the same man as before, no, not at all, in fact, if I didn't know better, I'd say something's missing, something that's just not there, that unknown something that's part of the soul and manifests in the eyes. It's gone. "Monty," to Belle's surprise, he addresses me first, "you know what you did. And you might be surprised, or maybe not, to learn that you succeeded. And you did it to us while she was nursing her sick mother."

"Kojo?" Belle's running her hands down the entire length of his chest and arms.

He's still staring at me, or rather straight through me. "I will not hit you, Monty, even though you deserve it, but only because I happen to know the one thing that will hurt you even more than physical pain."

Belle's striking blue eyes narrow on him. "Kojo? What is it?"

Finally, he tilts down his face to meet her gaze. "Arabella, let us go from this place." He holds out his hand and, with the colour of their fingers contrasting perfectly as they intertwine, Belle, the most beautiful girl in the world yelps with delight.

CHAPTER 11

Euphoria

ARABELLA

Montgomery trails us the entire walk home, crying his eyes out, pleading, begging, offering money to Kojo, to me, to us both if only we wouldn't go through with what he's suspecting we're about to. What Montgomery doesn't know is that neither he nor his friend Rupert possesses anywhere near enough money to change either of our minds about this, about what we're going to do just as soon as we arrive home.

"Please, don't do this," he cries with hands clasped out in front. It might have been funny if only it wasn't so pathetic.

"Montgomery," I say with barely any emotion because after what I've learned tonight I feel absolutely nothing, at least not for Montgomery, "we're going back to my room to have sex and there's nothing you can do to stop us, so the sooner you get used to the idea the better it will be for you."

Kojo's not finding it funny either. He seems different. But then, if Montgomery is crazy enough to arrange for me to be - ugh, I can't even find the words to think it, about what he conspired, let alone say it - even though he claims to be in love with me then I can't imagine what he's done to Kojo, his rival for my affections. Maybe he'll tell me, you know, later, after he's released his seed inside of me, and then I can bask in the relief of what very nearly came to be; me and Montgomery, ugh.

"Oh, God, no, you can't seriously be thinking of fucking this guy, Belle, no, you cant, you mustn't, I refuse to allow it, for the love of God, he's black!"

"Yup, he most certainly is," I tilt my head up to give this very large, muscular, black African an appreciative glance and immediately feel the warmth flood through my body. I'm also not surprised in the least that racism is another one of Montgomery's problems.

Montgomery dashes suddenly towards the resort's outdoor bar, briefly leaving me alone with Kojo, who's still not saying very much at all, and a minute later the ginger's running back holding out a handful of Ghanaian cedi. "Take it," he flaps the money in front of Kojo, "please, will you just take it. No? I can get more? So much more! Just please, don't do this!"

The side of Kojo's mouth slowly curls up. "I think I will enjoy this all the more for your pain."

"Why won't you take the money?" He turns to me. "Belle, you take it!"

"I don't want your money, sweet pea, what I want is to have sex with this big black stud."

His hands are in his hair, tugging, and several ginger strands fly away on the small breeze. "Fuck! Belle, listen to me, if you fuck this…this dirty nigger then you can forget about ever working in my art dealership. I hear Starbucks are hiring, you hear that, Starbucks will be your future. Hahaha, fuck this animal and you'll spend the rest of your life serving coffee to people like me."

I shrug. "I still want to have sex with this man."

He tugs more ginger from his scalp and again runs ahead towards our nearing chalet, in his haste almost tripping over himself.

"What now?" I can only muse. No matter what he does, he can only delay the inevitable, not stop it, as frustrating as it might be for me regardless because the anticipation has caused a serious build-up of juices down below.

We arrive on the patio and Montgomery's already there holding his key inside the lock, both his feet pressing against the door. There's a snap and he falls back on his behind. "Too late!" He declares, standing and wiping the dirt from his khakis. "I snapped the key inside the lock so now you can't get in."

The door opens from the inside and then Rupert's standing there scratching his head. "What's going on, did someone knock?"

"You stupid bastard!" Montgomery yells at his friend.

"Coming through," I bypass Rupert, dragging Kojo in afterwards, closely followed by the pest. "Goodnight," I call, "don't wait up."

Montgomery flails past us, coming to stop in front of my bedroom door and sinking down to the ground in a heap. "You're not doing it, I refuse to allow it." To think I came so close to allowing such a man to have his way with me. Now, the very thought of Montgomery biting down on my breasts and digitally entering me makes my skin crawl. What was I thinking? Oh, yeah, I was fooled, tricked, manipulated and for all I know probably drugged. "Let us pass."

"I will not, never!"

Kojo steps forward. "Get out of the way," he says calmly, though his voice is so gravelly that it holds a definite calm authority. "Now, Monty!" There's a moment's hesitation, but as soon as Kojo takes a single step forward, it's as though someone's lit a firework up Montgomery's arse and he's scurrying away on all-fours. I skip inside and hear Kojo's voice as he turns around to face the main room, "do not disturb us." The door closes and I have to reach considerably around him to apply the latch.

"Well, *I* certainly wouldn't disobey you." I'm suddenly very giddy but am steadied by Kojo's hands on my hips. I have to stand on my tippy-toes to smush my lips against his and the first thought that pops into my head is that not only is this the first time I've kissed Kojo but it's the first time I've kissed *any* black man. His lips are full, plump, and feel so much softer than that other person's I was kissing earlier.

We sink further into it as our breathing intensifies and I feel Kojo's organ changing shape from within his shorts. I reach down to give it a rub through the material, causing him to groan inside my mouth and my eyes to open wide in surprise. I don't want to pull away but feel that I must. "Well, aren't you packing a nice tool down there."

It's been a while since I've had sex. Study and rowing were my priorities these last five years, the Montgomery thing was short-lived, thank God, and other than that there was only Bradley who came close, though he turned out to be another disaster for reasons I don't want to even think about now. In fact, one might say that right now I'm kinda, sorta gagging for it.

Kojo responds by seizing my breasts and through the thin flowery dress his hands make me feel so small. His pupils enlarge as they fix on my globes that are wonderfully exposed by the dress's design, as well as my deep, generous cleavage that rises and falls with my every heavy breath. Kicking off my heels the drop in height makes me feel even smaller before Kojo, but I waste no time slipping the straps from my shoulders, allowing the dress to tumble to the floor from when his clutch immediately runs down my belly to settle on my hips, and then I'm being effortlessly lifted and placed on the bed.

Sliding my hands beneath my back, I unhook my bra as Kojo slips my underwear down my thighs and positions his face at my entrance. I arch back and let out a moan as his lips connect with my button, slowly at first, and then he's increasing pressure, tempo, and adding his tongue while I lose myself in a delicious blurry haze. I press down on the back of his head and feel his tongue work its way further inside of me. He reaches up to envelop a breast while I hold down his hand and push up with my hips. I'm just about to be overtaken by a wave of unstoppable ecstasy when he pulls away and comes to his feet, leaving me panting, unquenched and horny as fuck.

"Kojo!"

He tugs off his t-shirt to reveal his incredible body and as he moves down to unfasten his button, even the sinews in his deltoids are visible. There's the sound of his zip lowering and then he's tugging down his shorts, hastily following with his underwear before coming back to a stand. Obviously, my eyes are immediately drawn to his meat as my body can only spring immediately up from the bed, my hands wrapping around him like I was inspecting a prize zucchini at a farmer's market.

"Kojo!" I exclaim as my mouth fills with an ocean of saliva. "Didn't miss too many meals growing up, did you?" Losing my virginity had been painful enough but after a couple of times my body got used to the feeling of my first real boyfriend being inside of me. The problem is that he hadn't been built like *this!*

Now, Kojo grins down at me, a dark hand finding its way back to my breast while the other loses itself within clusters of blonde. "I will go slow."

I nod. "That might be a good idea." I'm still hungrily sliding my hands, both of them, up and down his more than generous length whilst being sure to spread around some of the pre-juice that's started to seep from the tip of his dark mushroom that's smooth as silk, black as charcoal, terribly angry looking and not a great deal smaller than my fist.

"That's enough," he shivers and tenses his body, "girl, you turn me on so much, we do not want to have an accident."

"Indeed not," because that would be the most terrible waste in the world. I recline back, bringing him down with me as I brace to receive his considerable bodyweight.

He transfers most of his load to one elbow placed beside my head as he reaches back to steer himself towards my entrance. A breath is forced from me as he knocks at the door, his bald dome attempting to prise apart my slit so that he can squeeze himself inside. I have to push up with my hips, spread my knees a little further apart and will myself to open before finally he's able to break through.

"Awwweee," we both sigh together, the most satisfying feeling in the world, for me that of a large man entering after so long, for him an impossibly tight snatch gripping him like a Chinese finger trap.

"Bella, you are so small," he attempts to push forwards but only hits another wall, "I love this feeling."

I push up with my hips, despite the pain willing him further inside. "It's not just me, you know, you're pretty damned large."

He grins again and reaches up to grab ahold of the mattress, hooking my jaw in the crack of his elbow. I hitch my knees further up and clasp my ankles around his back, hoping this angle will make his penetration easier. It does, and we both release a collective sigh as he begins slowly impaling me, inch after inch of dark meat, my body trembling as a trillion nerve endings react to this alien yet incredible feeling, signalling to my body to produce lubricant to further aid his push. I press down on his buttocks, solid like steel, and then he grunts into my ear when he's finally able to fully root himself.

I intensify my hold on him with both my arms and legs. "Let's just stay like this for a bit," I hiss, "just let me get used to this."

Our lips again connect as my cunt adjusts to being stretched and the pain slowly subsides. It's the most enjoyable and physically sensual few minutes of my life. When I can't take it anymore, I start moving against him, urging him to persist.

He pulls slowly out before pushing delightfully back inside, my pussy now feeling forlornly empty with every retraction before once again feeling fulfilled, complete, with his every forward thrust. He gathers pace, my fingers sinking into his flesh as he changes up his strokes; short, long, shallow, deeeeeeep, slow, fast. He reaches back and hooks his elbow beneath my knee, bringing it towards my chest and changing the spot that he hits, if anything deeper now as he continues pushing in and out. To my side, the mirror reveals our perfectly contrasting forms; large, strong and dark against feminine petite, supple and white.

Outside I can vaguely hear what's almost certainly Montgomery balling his eyes out, but not wanting to think about *that* right now, I instead take a deep inhalation of Kojo's deep, musky scent, pulling myself back into this wonderful reality that is the present as he continues plunging in and out of me.

It's not long before there's an unfamiliar humming emanating from my snatch and uterus before spreading towards my pelvic floor muscles, I mean, I know, or rather suspect what it is that's building inside of me but no man has ever intentionally achieved making me experience a vaginal orgasm before, so how can I be completely certain this wonderful sensation is about to…

And then a flood of warmth explodes throughout me as my entire body descends into a shivering rigid mass concentrated around my stretched out pussy that clenches hard around Kojo's incredible size. He fully hilts and pauses to enjoy the sensation of being gripped so tightly as my eyes roll back and my nails dig into his buttocks.

It takes a moment to come down but when I do I can only clamp my lips against Kojo's as I tighten the lock around his back with my ankles. Perhaps it's one of the reasons why, in comparison to other women, sex has never been quite so at the forefront of my mind. It's been enjoyable enough but never earth-shakingly orgasmic like this.

And all I want is more.

More!

More!

More!

Because I could so very easily become addicted to Kojo's manhood and how it makes my body come alive.

"My ears," Kojo laughs.

If I screamed then I was barely cognizant of it. Oh, poor, Montgomery. Thinking of him, I have an idea that I just can't resist. "Let's change positions."

He slowly pulls out and when he does there's a large opening where I used to be taut. I'm also very conscious to the fact he hasn't yet left his creamy deposit inside of me. That will soon be changing, I have little doubt about that.

I set up my phone on the bedhead, placing it in such a way that only my face is visible, along hopefully with part of a muscular black torso positioned as close behind as it's possible to get. A deep hum is emitted from Kojo when he realizes what I'm doing.

I set it to record and position myself on all-fours so that my entrance is presented for my lover. My lips are forced apart once more, my hips are seized and then Kojo's pushing back inside of me where he belongs. The way my teeth are pinching at my lower lip is in focus on the screen as my body butts forwards with every smack of Kojo's thighs against my arse, again and again, while I'm held in situ by strong hands, my flesh flushing red from the heat as sweat pricks at my forehead. As I watch Kojo fucking me from behind, there could not be a greater disparity between our two colours, not to mention physicalities, as this large and sexy man persists with his deep thrusts, penetrating so far inside of me that I'm sure my cervix is taking a beating. I let out a moan as he hits a sweet spot and a giant hand moves forwards to seize a heaving breast.

"Fuck, Bella, I am going to release inside of you soon." His voice is hoarse beyond description, and I can't wait to feel his sweet, sticky release.

I wiggle my hips to signal that he should continue, that he should not stop under any circumstances, not that he ever would, and as I feel my second climax start to swirl from the pit of my stomach and my flesh reddens in anticipation, his grip on my ass strengthens. My black lover lets out a deep growl as his entire body turns rigid and then this exceptionally strong and powerful man is pressing his hips as hard against my buttocks as his arms will allow, his penetration absolute, and then I can feel his seed releasing, gush after delectable gush of hot cum filling my every recess. I'm seized, finally, by my second climax that works to suck Kojo's seed deeper inside of me and then, as my eyes blur out, we collapse together on the bed in a hot, sticky embrace.

CHAPTER 12

Anguish

MONTGOMERY

I haven't slept at all and by the sounds of it neither have Kojo and Belle. Even after there's a lull in the awful noise coming from her bedroom, no doubt because they've exhausted themselves, I'm still not able to sleep.

It's not until the middle of the morning when finally a door opens and heavy footsteps on the wooden floor prompt me to throw the sheet from my eyes, only to be presented by a fully naked Kojo standing at the fridge. He removes the carton of milk I'd purchased yesterday at the resort shop and tips it back in a way that makes his biceps peak, the heavy muscles in his back bulge and his buttocks clench. He makes an obnoxious chugging sound and then turns around so that I get a view of his drooping cock that catches between his thighs as he now plods in my direction, his visible milk moustache the antithesis to his flesh. Fuck, but is that how Belle's flesh contrasted against his when he was humping her?

I turn away. How ever am I supposed to look at him, or her, in the eye ever again?

He stops close to my wicker couch and I feel his gaze

burning into me, his judgement. "What happened to your hair, Monty, my friend?"

I glance down to the ground and find the large clumps of ginger that last night in my turmoil I'd tugged out. I decide not to answer. I have nothing to say to him anyway.

Kojo sighs. "Do not destroy yourself over this, Monty, there will be other women for you in this life. For me? Perhaps not."

I remain staring forwards, his enormous quads and his obscene dick in the top of my field of vision. By God, but that thing has to be nine inches in the soft, at least, and thicker than the fat end of a beer bottle. Surely he can't grow much more than that? Surely. Surely!

When I don't respond he continues. "Hopefully you will learn from this, Monty, and become a better man for the experience." He yawns for a long time. "Contrary to what you might believe, I do not wish you anymore hurt than I have already caused."

"Kojo…" Belle sighs from her bedroom.

"Ah, it looks like I am being summoned. Monty, perhaps it would be best if you do not remain so close to listen." The floor shudders as he steps back towards the bedroom and closes the door after him. A few seconds later there's a solitary "aaaaahhhh," as I imagine he's entering her and then the moans recommence in earnest as the slapping of his thighs against her arse penetrates through the wall.

That's another thing about niggers, they love doggy style, for some reason, I suspect because it's more animalistic, primitive, whereas I'd always pictured myself at least facing Belle while I was making love to her. Niggers and white people, we're just not the same and quite frankly, what they're doing right now is an abomination.

The other door opens and then Rupert drags himself out with a face like a slapped behind, no doubt because I'm not the only one who spent the entirety of last night balling my eyes out. That Milly had failed to return home had barely even registered with me. "You heard anything from her?" God, but he sounds as broken as I am. I make the smallest of head shakes and then he's pottering about aimlessly whilst tactfully not mentioning the obvious grunts, wails and screams coming from Belle's room. "You'll tell me if you get a message?"

I nod and watch as he returns to his room to languish before deciding to check my phone in the unlikely event Milly did send me a message. "What the...?" There's a video from Belle that by the timestamp was sent during the night. I can't think what the fuck it might be but open it anyway only to be immediately presented with a close-up of Belle's face deep in the throes of orgasm while a large black torso looms ominously behind. It plays on a loop, about five seconds of footage like one of those GIF files, and shows absolutely nothing that might be considered even softcore porn, not even a tit, though the implication is definitely clear, that Belle's being brought off by a big black dick stuffed deep inside of her. And quite obviously, she's sent this to me to inflict pain.

My mouth gapes in disgust because my boner's straining so hard that it feels like it's about to explode. "What the fuck?" It's now that I'm reminded it's been twenty days since I last used a tissue to ejaculate and since it no longer looks like I'll be loosing my rancid accumulation inside of Belle, as hoped, then... "no!" I shake my head. "Not to this!"

"Ah, fuck...yes, yes, yeeeesssss, Kojo!!!"

I can only glare down at the little lump making the sheet poke up and even as my entire body is shaking with confusion, disarray and no small amount of disgust, I'm unable to prevent my hand from sliding down my body before delving beneath my waistband and wrapping around my cock. "What is the fucking matter with me?"

"Oh...oh, Kojo, yes, yes, yes!!!"

I'd thought I was completely out of tears but one rolls

down my cheek regardless as I stare at the video and commence tugging. It's less than ten seconds before I'm spilling all over my khakis, underwear, the sheet and there's probably a whole vanilla pudding cup's worth of jizz staining the cushions too. I manage to shut down my screen and wipe the remnants from my hand just as the bedroom door again opens.

It's Belle who steps wobbly into the room wearing only Kojo's white shirt from last night, the hems at the bottom extending adequately past her contaminated snatch while the top two buttons are left undone to expose her tainted cleavage. "Whoa, careful, girl, your legs might give out and you haven't eaten."

I've stopped shaking a bit but there's nothing I can do to stop my top lip from curling up to reveal teeth. "Cunt," I mutter under my breath.

"Oh, now-now, sweet pea, don't be like that," she's literally clinging to the fucking wall as she edges towards the fridge, "did you get the little present I sent?"

I ignore her. I'd get up and leave if it wasn't for the awful mess I was hiding beneath the sheet.

She lets go of the wall and forgoes sustenance temporarily to make a detour in my direction, hobbling across the floor while using the support column and table for assistance until she reaches the couch. "I thought you'd enjoy that, you know, since you like taking photos of Kojo and me together so much."

There's nothing I can do to stop my face from twisting away but her present silence only prompts me to question if she knows, or at least suspects, a little more than I'd like her to right now.

She barks suddenly. "Oh, you didn't. Please tell me you didn't." She yelps. "You did?"

"Leave me alone," I growl at the slut, pretty much confirming that I did just wank off to the image of Belle getting fucked by Kojo. If only my mind was working right now, I might have been able to deny it a little better.

"You did," she tips back to laugh, "well, enjoy it, sweet pea, because that's the closest you're ever going to get." She slinks around the back of the couch and leans down close to my ear. "You fool. He wasn't even interested in me until you destroyed the relationship with his fiancée." Her hands are on my shoulders now and despite everything the lump beneath the sheet is quick to return. "You did it to yourself," she hisses into my ear before kissing me once on the cheek, "which is why I must thank you because that was the best sex of my entire life and there's more to come. A lot more, hopefully." She pulls away and walks back round to my front, her voice returning to normal. "Oh, and by the way, Kojo told me about your little micro dick." She shakes her head. "It's no wonder you're so insecure. Kojo's, on the other hand…" she closes her eyes and shivers.

"Bella," comes the deep, gravelly voice from the opened doorway, "I will get Cedric to make a delivery. Come back to bed."

"Coming, my lover," she turns briefly back from the bedroom for long enough to address me one last time, placing her hands on my knees and leaning slowly down to expose her sumptuous cleavage that, even now, I still can't help but wish to bury my face in, "I'd say he's packing a python, at least."

CHAPTER 13

One Month Later

MONTGOMERY

It was thought best for the four of us to get some much needed space from each other, at least for a few weeks. To that end I found a cheap hotel in Accra where I'm constantly roused by beggars and streetwalkers because, well, for obvious reasons, while Rupert remained in the luxury chalet paid for by his father. From what I hear, Kojo managed to hook Belle up with an empty resort chalet at an extreme discount and where I've little doubt she spends the majority of her free time getting all her holes filled by her well-endowed African lover, the very thought of which is a constant source of anxiety for me. Which leaves Milly, who sent a car to collect her belongings after having taken up residence in a room in Aburi with her new best friend Cathy, or so she says.

Four weeks after our group's falling out, Rupert and I are finally back at the village determined to see out the rest of this charity thing. No, that's a lie, the reason he's back is to try patch things up with Milly, while I have my very own contingency to think about.

"What the feck?" It's Jimmy who's first to greet the both of us on our return after a month away from the place.

I throw up my hands. "Yes, I know, sorry-sorry, we've had problems."

"No, it's not that," he shakes his head and wraps his hand around my right arm, "have you been juicing?"

Well, I hadn't been prepared for *that* being the first thing he'd mention, and my surprised reaction gives away the fact that I am indeed juicing. "Let's not make a big deal out of it, ok?"

He's giving me a strange look now, checking out the rest of my body. "And what kind of defective roids are these?" This is no doubt in reference to the fact the only thing that seems to have grown is my right bicep, almost certainly on account of the amount of wanking I've been catching up on whilst staring at that video. Rupert had also earlier mentioned that he thought my right arm looked twice the size of my left. Man, I've got problems, but asking Ingrid out for a drink in Accra might be just the cure that I need right now.

"Where's the supermodel doctor?" I ask Jimmy.

He gives me a knowing glance. "She's taking a few days off, so…" he thrusts a shovel in each of our hands, "you'll have to wait until after your shift, won't you."

We get to digging and I'd be lying if I said I was glad to be back toiling in the awful heat. About an hour before lunch there's a loud cheer that comes from the main building but such things are not unheard of around here so we ignore it and continue with our work. It's not until an hour later that Jimmy receives a ping and then sits on a nearby tree stump to watch a video on his phone.

"Hey, lads, you might want to come and take a look at this." Something in his voice prompts Rupert and me to give each other a look before joining him to see what's up. "Cathy's shooting a livestream from the feckin village," he says as we gather around to watch.

"Guys," she begins in her American twang while holding her cell at the end of a long selfie stick, her belly now swollen more than ever, "I've got some awesome news to bring you all." It looks like she's shooting the video from the outdoor eating area and there's the usual crowd of women gathered around. Belle's there sitting back wafting a fan at her face, which sends various emotional pangs shooting through my body. The camera pans to the attractive girl in a flowing white dress sitting beside her.

"It's Milly!" Rupert yelps, and it occurs to me that he's not seen his girlfriend, or rather *former* girlfriend, in as long as I haven't seen Belle. Indeed, I can only imagine the trauma and turmoil my friend has been suffering these past few weeks.

"Come on," Cathy nudges, "tell us all your awesome news."

"Well…" Milly flushes and glances briefly at whoever's off-screen standing to her right, "I've kind of, sort of, missed my period."

"What?" Rupert barks before almost falling into me. I have to use my hands to steady myself and keep him upright.

Cathy makes a delighted squeal. "You … you mean … you're carrying a little brother or sister to my own soon-to-be born?"

Milly tilts her chin up and pushes out her chest. "Looks like it."

Another cheer comes from the village and immediately the screen lights up with hearts, fireworks and Facebook's trademark thumbs-up emoji. Even as the bile starts working its way up from my stomach the comments are coming in thick and fast…

'Wonderful.'

'Another beautiful baby.'

'Love is love.'

'I can't wait to make my way to Aburi.'

Rupert's hands are in his short brown fuzz. "What the fuck is this? She … she told me … she told me she wants to start with the silly fucking opera thing."

I'm shaking my head, it's all so hard to believe, and neither do I need to ask who it is that's succeeded in fertilizing the same egg we'd so painstakingly conspired to fertilize with Rupert's seed. Women! And yet they fail to see why every successful civilization throughout the entirety of history has sought to control their sexual freedom.

The camera pans back to Belle. "And you have some news of your own?" The horrid little tart says, giving me an immediate bad feeling.

Belle nods whilst failing to hide her enormous grin. "I've missed my period too."

In an instant, I'm throwing up into the ditch, again and again, hurl after toxic, nasty fucking hurl, my entire fucking breakfast and probably last night's dinner too. I wipe my mouth and then, in a blur, the three of us are charging for the main building.

"Milly!" It's Rupert who arrives first in the courtyard and without even stopping to think about what he's doing he's falling to his knees right in front of Milly. "Please, please, please, my love, I'm so sorry I tried to get you pregnant, I should never have attempted such a thing, please, we can still be together, can't we? Here..." he tugs the small black box from his pocket and holds the ring up to Milly, "please, we can get married and I'll take care of you and the baby, we can be a family and..."

It's the silence that checks me, in case I was about to do something similar with Belle, that and the fact everybody's staring at my friend. Last but by no means least, Cathy's getting all of this on her livestream. It's only now that for the first time I notice Winston leaning casually against a nearby wall, a curious eyebrow cocked as he strokes his stubble.

"Please, Milly," Rupert's arms are wrapped around Milly's legs now, "I don't care who the father is, I just want to be with you. The three of us, forever!"

Finally, the shocked silence breaks when Winston

chuckles, followed by Cathy, and then there are a few dozen men, women and children all laughing even as the pictures are beamed around the world.

I back away, cautious to stay out of the camera's line of sight, as well as to avoid Belle's eye contact, and then I'm slipping around the corner taking a deep breath, thankful that unlike Rupert I just avoided the ultimate humiliation.

Ingrid!

That's right! There's still Ingrid! And thank God for that, for her, because not all women are completely fucking worthless trashbag whores. "Old Mrs Tettay's," I declare and quickly head across the dust-strewn ground for her mud hut. I don't know what I'm going to say or do when I get there, I guess right now all I need is for my faith in womanhood, in humanity, to be restored, though as I close on the door I'm thinking that perhaps the two of us could leave this terrible place together, right fucking now, or else I'll go insane.

I bang on the door, the thin piece of sheet metal that counts for one rattles loud. "Ingrid!" I bang again, the door swings open and I find myself facing an enormous African wearing only a skirt of leaves along with a necklace of beads and bones.

"Amekae nènye eye nuka dim nèle," he shouts in some incomprehensible tribal dialect. His ears are stretched out by discs, red stripes are painted on his shiny bald head and there's the most ungodly stench of body odour I've ever experienced in my life. He shouts again and steps forwards, prompting me to step quickly away.

"Sorry," I hold up my hands, quickly glancing left and right for Mrs Tettay's shack and the beautiful blonde girl waiting for me inside, "wrong place."

"Otumbo?" Calls the feminine voice from behind the enormous man. "Come back to bed." A white arm hooks around his front and delves beneath the leaf skirt to mischievously grab ahold of whatever lurks underneath and then there's a gasp when Ingrid sees me.

"The fuck?" My mouth plunges open as I feel something else about to drop.

Ingrid straightens and her hand wilts from the African's cock. "Monty?"

"Ingrid? What are you…" I back away and continue backing away, all the way to the Humvee.

"Sir?" The driver says.

"Home," I mumble, monotone, "take me the fuck home, right now."

Epilogue: Three Years Later

"**A**re you sure you really want to go through with this?" I ask Rupert for what's probably the tenth time in as many days, after all, as best man it's my job to look out for him.

"Yes!" He repeats without a shred of doubt in his mind. "The two of us," he means himself and Milly, of course, "have discussed it many times and we really want to make a go of it." He glances across at his son, for lack of a better word, Chiyembekezo, which apparently means *hope*, and smiles with pride as he plays on the chapel's grass with the other kids. He's bigger than all of the white children surrounding him, despite being younger than some.

It had taken a while for my friend's parents to get used to the idea of not only their son and Milly getting back together, but that she'd also, finally, accepted his earlier proposal of marriage, and the truth is that I'm still not sure whether Rupert Senior is completely ok with it, for obvious reasons, but with no other kids of his own then it looks like he has no option but to pin all of what remains of his hopes on Rupert Junior.

"And what about kids of your own?" I can't help but ask.

Rupert gives me a rebuking look. "I already have at least *one* of my own, Monty," he shakes his head, "but to answer your question, because I know what it is you're really thinking, then the answer's *no*, at least not for the moment, because Milly's decided she finally wants to start with the London Festival Opera, after all."

"Great!" I nod. "Well, she's delayed her career long enough, so why not?" It's funny how things can work out and how people can change their minds.

Rupert goes on to explain that he'll be taking care of Chiyembekezo whilst she travels the world singing and dancing, the very thing we'd once tried so hard to thwart. We step closer to where the children are playing and Rupert picks up his son. "So it looks like it'll be just you and me for a while, ain't that right, Kezo?"

The child babbles and I tickle him under the chin, a remarkably cute young man with dark eyes, woolly black hair and a grin like Winston. If he turns out to be an only child like Rupert then this little one will be set to inherit billions and enough land to feed all of Africa ten times over.

I wait for Rupert to place the child down before asking. "And how's the sex these days, if you don't mind my asking?"

He smiles and I can instantly see there's been some kind of a change in him. "Like rabbits, Monty."

"That's great, big guy!" I slap him on the back, happy things are working out, and decide not to say that she's undoubtedly pussy bombing him until such time as the wedding's out of the way and her child's, as well as her own, future, is secured. No, I've turned over a new leaf, life has taught me many lessons, and I'm a better person these days. It's for this reason that I also don't ask if she's still making him rubber up, although the answer to that is obvious so I don't need to ask anyway. After all, what choice does Milly have if she's striking out with her career because undoubtedly she'll still be allergic to contraceptives, not to mention anti-abortion on moral grounds. I'm absolutely sure she won't cheat on Rupert whilst travelling with a troupe of fit, muscular dancers and he's back home looking after her child, just as I'm also sure she'll want another child with Rupert at some point in the future.

We're at Carrington Hall, one of the de Beaumont family's many country estates and the beautiful wedding ceremony passes without any issues. I make my best man's speech and have the three hundred attendees in stitches with stories about drinking, Oxford and yet more drinking. From my vantage point at the top table I'm able to spot Ingrid seated beside her Swedish husband, their African child on his lap, and never did she look more beautiful than now, and neither was there a more perfect looking family. From what I hear she married another doctor and owing to their important careers they've decided to have no kids of their own. I wish them nothing but the very best of luck.

Jimmy's here too and after having dropped the idea of becoming a priest, he's brought along his fiancée, Beatrice. She has closely cropped ginger hair, similar to his, is covered in tattoos, piercings, and is presently fagged out in a special chair we had to winch in from the nearby British Airways maintenance hangar. Aye, it's funny how life can work out. I remember the days when the only man a lady like Beatrice could expect to attract would be a recently arrived immigrant from sub-Saharan Africa. These days those immigrants are taking most of our best women, leaving only the likes of Beatrice for us. Oh, well, at least Jimmy's happy, I suppose.

"Great speech, Monty," it's Belle who's sitting beside me at the top table.

I twist towards her and smile. "Thanks, that means a lot." I'm glad things are amicable between us, which says much about how I've grown these last three years, that I'm no longer bitter about what happened the last time I saw her. Of course, it helps to know she's a struggling single mum living in a rundown part of Glasgow, abandoned by her family and barely able to make ends meet, and that she's putting her tits out on OnlyFans to her fifteen subscribers is the icing on the cake. Aye, all this helps me feel a little better, despite my personal growth, I cannot tell a lie. As for my personal growth, I persisted with the weightlifting, deciding to ditch the steroids in favour of putting in the work and being natural, and having spent the first year losing the excess blubber, over the next two years I've built some quality muscle. It had been an awesome feeling when Belle first saw me after so long and made a double-take.

"So, um, how's the art dealership going?" Like she doesn't already know everything about my art dealership. She shuffles closer in her seat, lines already starting to appear on her face at the tender age of twenty-six. "I read an article the other week saying you sold an original John Constable for twenty million quid."

I shrug, "well, it was a team effort." No, that's a lie. It was all me who generated the media frenzy after discovering the 'fake' Hay Wain painting was indeed genuine. Ka-ching! And now Monty's is one of the most famous and reputable art dealerships in Europe.

She hums and her foot makes contact with mine beneath the table. "It was always one of my regrets, you know, not taking you up on your offer."

I turn to face her, unable to hide my smile. "Which offer are you talking about specifically?"

She swipes a cluster of brittle, discoloured blonde away from her eyes. "Both."

My head jerks back in feigned surprise. "Both? Wow, I don't know what to say, Belle."

Her hand moves to my knee. "Well, perhaps after the reception we might discuss them both again over a bottle of champagne?"

I pucker my lips and adjust my Roberto Romano tie that cost fifty grand. "That would be wonderful, Arabella, except," I now point to the staggeringly beautiful woman with long brown hair watching from table eight, "I'm not so sure my wife would like it very much." I pat her on the shoulder and stand. "Have a good life, Belle."

"Is that the girl?" Louise asks when I arrive back at the table.

I nod. "She's shoddy cloth beside you, my love." I kiss her on the lips and know that I mean it. Belle had been an infatuation, nothing more, but with Louise it's love. Pure and simple. Arabella turned me into a monster but with Louise, I try my hardest every day to be the best person I can possibly be, as tacky as it sounds but it's true. I'm succeeding, bit by bit, I think, and it's all thanks to her.

"She looks unhappy, I hope things work out for her." My wife threads her arm inside of mine and tugs herself closer. An up-and-coming actress, we'd met when she turned up one day in the dealership looking to invest in some art. I'd shoved both Archibald and Horace aside, telling them to go for lunch, and not only had she taken a portrait of London in the snow but she'd stolen my heart as well. Six months later we were married. She now glances athwart my body and gestures with her chin. "Is that the man?"

I've been well aware all evening of Kojo's location seated at table fifteen with the old Aburi gang, as far from the top table, specifically Belle, as possible. "It is," I say matter of fact and feel a stir in my belly, "looks like you spotted him right away, my love."

"Well, from your description, it was obvious."

I glance at my wife, hoping to gauge her reaction. So far she's given very little away.

"You're wanting me to say what I'm thinking." You see what I mean? She gets me.

I shuffle against the seat. "Well?"

"He's..." she's looking attentively in Kojo's direction, "exactly as you described. Big. Black. Muscular. What else is there for me to say?" We're both very still and silent for a few moments and I try to decide if I can feel my wife stirring, hear her humming, if even only slightly. It's all in *my* head, I recognize, not hers. Finally, she breaks the silence. "He received the card you left?"

Something that might be described as a sad grunt is omitted from me. "I don't know." And, I'm thinking, the only way I'll ever find out for sure is by biting the bullet and going over there to ask him. Sure enough, Kojo hasn't yet approached me, and neither have we so much as made eye contact all evening which, unfortunately, might answer things for me. Seeing him here, though, not just in England but in London, is bringing back all kinds of memories, of painful emotions that's making my cock strain within my best trousers.

"And he's definitely not with that Belle girl?" My wife enquires, actually sounding curious.

I shake my head. "No, no, my love, the little fling they had lasted only as long as he needed to make his way through an entire hen party." Which is one way of ending a budding relationship, even if it succeeded in producing one son. I haven't seen Kwamena at the wedding so I can only presume he's been left with friends up in Scotland. Obviously, I'd hurt this man more than I knew at the time. Or cared. But I feel bad about it now. Truly. If this world blesses us each with only one very special person to love then I'd found mine in Louise, even if I'd cost Kojo his, despite the friendship he'd once tried to offer me.

My wife hums. "I can see why women would like him."

I look straight at her, unable to stop the side of my lips from slowly curling upwards, and her hold around my arm intensifies.

It's more than an hour into the dancing, and several

drinks, before finally I find the balls to approach Kojo. He's standing with a man from Aburi I recognize but whose name I've long forgotten, and his face perks immediately.

"Hello, Monty, my friend." He turns briefly to the other man. "Would you excuse me for a few moments." Kojo returns to me, holds out his hand, and I note how wonderful it feels for my own hand to be so thoroughly swallowed by his. These past years I've been keeping close tabs on Kojo. The best thing about his recent history, a mere three months ago to be precise, is that he placed second, again, in the Man Ghana bodybuilding competition. To look at the man there's little doubting he deserved to win it. From what I can gather he still works as a lifeguard at the resort, though there's no doubt whatsoever in my mind that he makes money on the side by *taking care* of rich Western women who arrive on his patch. Still, citing the cost of such a trip to England, initially he'd turned down Rupert and Milly's invite, which had bothered me immensely. Later, I'd found his website where he sells autographed images posing in trunks, and had paid two and a half thousand dollars for a double biceps shot he priced at a mere ten. Shortly after he told Milly he could now afford the trip and would be glad to attend, just so long as they could keep him apart from Belle.

"It is good to see you." His voice is deep as ever and brings back a flood of memories, both painful and frustrating. If he still harbours any animosity towards me then you wouldn't know it.

We spend time chatting, small talk mostly, though every time I try steering the conversation towards Belle and their son in an effort to move it on to the very subject of sex, he frustratingly brings it back to my art dealership. He looks good, incredible, even, in the suit he's wearing, and I feel a guilty stir in my loins every time he bends his elbow and stretches his sleeve. Even through the jacket his pectorals are beyond thick, his collar struggles to contain his trapezius muscles and the wide expanse of his lats bestows the additional illusion of an impossibly trim waist. He still hasn't mentioned the card I left for him, which again is frustrating. From not far away I can sense my beautiful wife paying close attention to the interaction, which I'm happy for her to do, of course, and I hope she's making comparisons between the two of us; Kojo's six and a half foot frame to my five foot and eight inches, my soft and graceful chin to his rugged, masculine jaw, and his hard, jet black exterior to my comparatively soft and pink flesh covered in freckles. Aesthetically, we could not be more different, and I'd love nothing more than to know what's going through Louise's mind right now, seeing us so close together, just talking. Most importantly, is she tempted?

"I hope you're enjoying England," I remark. "If you don't mind my asking, where exactly are you staying?"

He shrugs. "Wonderful country and I like the people. I am staying in a hotel in Whitechapel."

"Whitechapel?" I shake my head. "Oh, that's no good. You never heard of Jack the Ripper? Not to mention the long taxi ride. No. A friend of ours? You should have been put in a room here. I can fix that for you, if you'd like?"

"I would not want to be any trouble?"

"Kojo," I touch his arm and feel a twinge from the solid musculature beneath his suit jacket, "you're our friend, it would be my pleasure."

His face is typically stony and hard to read. "Monty, my friend, are you married?"

I almost choke on my beer. I have only a second to decide if this is yet more small talk or if this man has done the masculine thing and just gotten straight to the bloody point. Either way, I'm extraordinarily keen to jump in with the answer.

"Yes!" Beads of sweat trickle down my back. "I'm married." I twist around and point to Louise looking beyond immaculate in a devilish red dress that displays only enough of her ample cleavage to remain classy. "You see her, over there?"

Kojo's eyes widen, it does not escape my attention. "What, the lady in red?" He actually sounds not only surprised, but impressed. You never know, but this might just end up working out.

"Beautiful, isn't she?" I intone my words in a way that makes it clear I'm asking for his opinion which, of course, I am.

He's still gazing in Louise's direction, and I can't blame him. "Monty, you are the luckiest man in the world."

I nod. "Thank you, and I know, yes, I am."

He now looks back at me. "So why would you leave such a card for me at reception, Monty, my friend?"

I'm caught more than a little off-guard by the direct nature of the question, though I'm not sure what else I was expecting from Kojo. The truth is I've never been able to fully explain it. I'm not sure if it was seeing him together with Belle that forever changed me, if it's the pain I enjoy, the thought of humiliation, or if I'm just some kind of a sick freak. Maybe, deep down, I feel guilt for what I did to him and his fiancée and, in my own strange way, desire only to make things right, somehow. All I do know for sure is that I'd love nothing more than to see the man who already broke my heart once do it all over again, only this time with my wife. I know I'm incapable of putting all this into words, especially in the heat of the moment to the very man in question, so all I can do is weakly say, "I just think it's something I'd like to see, that's all."

His face is terribly unreadable and I feel my heart sinking. "I don't think it would be a good idea, Monty."

My hand is back on his arm and his gaze moves down to my fingers. "Don't be so hasty with your decision, please, um, how about … how about I introduce you to her?" My brain is frantically scouring for the right words to say. "Perhaps, um, if the two of you were to go for a walk outside, have a brief chat, maybe, then perhaps you could decide if it's something you…" I leave it there, having made my point.

And then, almost as though my wife's ears have been burning, Louise appears in all her elegance and offers her dainty hand to Kojo. "Can I meet the man who's stolen my husband?" Such is her way, she makes it sound like, for a few moments at least, that Kojo's the most important man in the world.

Kojo actually laughs and I must admit, I'd have laughed myself if I wasn't so bloody dishevelled right now. "Mrs Monty, I do not think I could ever steal your husband away from *you*." It's a compliment, for sure, which is positive, and too right he should be complimenting Louise. My wife has been compared to a young Ava Gardner in looks, Cate Blanchett in talent and Audrey Hepburn in charm. I've seen all kinds of men, women too, turn to jelly under her gaze, her spell. I once watched her charm a gay movie director, who hated me, into casting her as the lead in a drama series. When Louise turns it on, men like Kojo don't stand a chance. Or so I hope.

"Well, that's a relief." She threads her arm inside of mine and I can't help but notice the way her pupils have dilated. She's also thrusting out her breasts, though not so much that it's overly noticeable.

The big African's dark eyes feast on her, particularly the small amount of cleavage she's displaying. Damn it, but if only he'd accept our invitation then he'd get to see a heck of a lot more than the crest of my wife's boobs, the nape of her slender neck and the curves of her hips in a Valentino Esposito dress.

There's silence for a few moments as the rest of the room dissolves into a haze. All three of us know what's going on here and there's definitely a palpable anxiety, a sexual tension, even, existing in this little bubble. It's so bad that my head is completely scrambled, my usual quick wits diminished, and I fear that if I don't salvage things soon then this wonderful opportunity might soon slip through my fingers. Forever. Fortunately, I'm getting the definite impression that I'm not the only man here who's lost his wits.

Finally, it's my wife who breaks the silence. "It's so nice to meet you, Kojo," it's only now that I notice their hands are still connected, and have been this whole time, "I shall leave you and Monty to catch up and … *maybe*," she says open-endedly, "we'll meet again soon." She doesn't leave it sounding like a question, I notice, more a statement. *It's his choice.* She then gives me a fleeting smile before turning and stepping out the reception room towards the stairs and our suite.

Kojo's gaze lingers on the curvature of my woman's thighs and arse for as long as mine. "Monty, you are crazy."

I nod, fully in agreement. "Just promise me you'll think about it?"

"You are crazy!"

"We're in 301, it's the best room in the entire place apart from the honeymoon suite."

"You are crazy!"

"Look, as promised, I'll secure a room for you here but consider not using it, alright?" I hold out my hand, which he takes only after hesitating. "Room 301."

"Crazy."

I back away. "Please, just think about it."

"Is he coming?" It's the first thing my wife asks as soon as I enter our suite. She reclines back on our bed having since changed into a thirty thousand pound Chiara Lombardi negligee, its lace hems unbuttoned exposing the insides of her sumptuous breasts and enough thigh I can almost see her juicy snatch. It's the most scintillating sight in the entire fucking world and for a certain large, dark African not to call, now, tonight, when she's looking like this would be the biggest fucking waste in the world. There's a large glass of red wine on the table beside her which, evidently, she feels she'll need should Kojo decide to make my dreams come true.

I exhale and sound as disappointed as I feel. "I give it fifty-fifty." Which is saying something. He *saw* my wife, after all, he fucking *met* her. No, he couldn't take his fucking eyes off her. I refuse to believe that any hot-blooded man could withstand being in Louise's proximity for any period of time whatsoever and not become completely fucking infatuated.

She pats the space beside her. "Monty, come."

I climb on the mattress and lean against the bedhead beside her, inhale her smell and immediately feel myself growing. "You don't have to worry," I preempt what I know she's about to say.

"I know."

"If he does decide to come and ... whatever happens ... I'll never abandon you."

"I know that too." She's looking at me with an eyebrow half raised. She knows there's something I want to ask.

I savour the moment. "Did you like him?"

She sighs. "Honestly?"

I nod. "As we always are with each other."

Her lips pucker. "You know I'm not into black guys..."

"Right..."

"But..."

"Yes?"

She arches her back, again making her breasts push up and I don't even think she's aware she's doing it. "He's definitely one of the better looking black men I've seen." I remain silent, hoping she'll elaborate. As usual, my wife does not disappoint. "And he's not just black, Monty, I mean, he's *really* black. He's blaaaaaack-black."

I stir against the bed. "That he is."

"He has a photogenic face," which is my wife's way of saying she finds him physically attractive without having to actually say it, "very masculine features, strong jaw, friendly eyes."

"Yes."

"He's tall, Monty, six-five, six-six, at least. Aren't you worried that, I mean, aren't you worried he might be, you know, *in* proportion? Or is that what you're hoping for?"

I nod. "I already know he's *in* proportion, or *larger*, if anything." This is new information for Louise and I feel a stab of guilt for having kept it from her.

She gives me a look and I'm not sure what she's thinking. It bothers me. *Who did I marry here? Is he gay? What other secrets is he keeping from me?* Finally, she says, "and aren't you worried things might never be the same afterwards? For *us*, I mean."

"You mean," I angle down towards her beautiful vagina, still vice-tight despite the many thousands of times I've made love to her, "down there?"

She shakes her head, her expression not changing, a slight rebuke. "No, Monty, I mean up there," she taps my head with a finger.

I roll my eyes and shrug. "I don't know."

"You don't know? And yet you're convinced you want to see this big, black African man with enormous slabs of muscle who's also enormous in other places plough your wife?"

"That's right," I nod and show my palms. "I … I can't stop thinking about it." Even now I'm imagining Kojo's dick pumping in and out of my wife's cunt as she screams his name. My belly stirs and somehow I avoid rubbing myself. Truth is that if my wife was to rub me off right now, spilling my seed and ridding my head of all these scheming chemicals, I might well call this whole thing off. Well, for a day, perhaps, or less, and then I'd be assailed by these same treacherous thoughts all over again. I've always instinctively hated the very thought of black men being with our women and it's perhaps this that has something to do with the way I am now. My worst fears becoming an actual fucking sexual kink, and it's this that I simply cannot explain.

Her hand is on my knee, she knows that if she was to just touch me a little bit higher then I'd be on her in an instant, ravaging her, and then this moment would pass. She knows this. And that she's not, even now, aggressively seizing my cock tells me that she wants this too, she wants to have sex with Kojo, perhaps not as much as I want the two of them to have sex as I watch, but she wants it all the same, and it drives me both anxious and crazy in equal measure. Her tongue runs across her dry lips. "I brought a morning-after pill, of course, as you kept on reminding me."

I nod. "Good." We both want kids. *Our* kids! For real. Unlike some other people I could mention. And now that Louise has finished her latest movie *Starry Eyes*, there's no time like the present, especially considering her next role involves actually getting pregnant. As long as we plan this correctly then everything should work out perfectly for us, her career, and our future family. It's just a pity that this wonderful opportunity, brought by Milly and Rupert getting married, is happening now, rather than two or three months before when my wife was still on the pill. To top things off she's ovulating this very moment, hence the morning-after pill that will turn out to be essential. Yes, it'll mean wasting this precious egg, along with an opportunity of realizing our plans and hopes, though on balance I'm not about to miss this once in a lifetime chance with Kojo when the timing will still be pretty great next month too.

Another short silence. "Really, Monty, I've tried to understand this." Her hand is in my ginger hair now. *Is it far from my cock intentionally?* "You're insecure, is that it? You think that because I ... *look* the way I do that you don't deserve me?" She was uncomfortable saying that, my wife is unduly modest for a girl of her calibre. "You think that supposedly I'm out of your league so therefore you must make offerings of better looking, better endowed men, is that it?"

I know I've married a corker and that I'm probably the luckiest man in the world, though crass as it might sound, I've always considered us evenly matched; her looks, the three hundred million pounds and counting I own in assets. "It's not that."

She shakes her head. "Then you just want to see your pretty, young, and fertile wife getting ridden by a bull."

I nod. "Closer, I'm sure." I flap my hands. "Anyway, it'll all be for nought if he fails to show." Merely saying the words is enough for the disappointment to flood my body. Louise, I note, also pouts.

Three slow knocks at the door sends a rush of blood to my head. The two of us stare silently at each other until, finally, I'm able to shake away the fog and then I'm on my feet, dashing for the door and staring through the peephole. I turn back to Louise. "It's him." Fuck! I knew it. No man on earth would turn down no-strings sex with my wife. No man!

She flops back on the bed with both hands in her hair, exhaling loudly.

I'm back at the peephole. Kojo's staring left then right, his face a perfect contrast to the white painted walls that frame him. My God, but even now he looks impossibly large. Tall. Thick. And black! I'm suddenly very nervous and even though it's far from too late to back out, I wouldn't do so for the world.

I open the door. "Kojo!"

He silently nods, his eyes dipping slightly in disappointment, presumably because I'm the one who answered the door and not my wife. His dark eyes look beyond me but Louise is hidden by the angle of the wall. "Monty."

I take a deep breath and open the door fully, placing my body against it so that Kojo can squeeze past. He does slowly and I get a dose of his musky African scent that brings back memories of being carried across his broad shoulders, of sunburn and mental torment. I close the door after him and apply the lock, which causes him to twist around briefly. He still hasn't advanced further into our opulent room to where my wife's waiting.

I cough into a closed fist and have to squeeze past him. "Come, please."

He follows and his gaze immediately finds Louise, who's perching on the edge of the bed now, not seductive at all, in fact, if anything, by the way she's taking up so little space she appears reserved and demure, and yet it's the most seductive thing I've ever seen regardless. Yes, I know that's a fucking contradiction but who fucking cares right now? As I said, my wife has it, even if she knows how to fake it.

"Hello again," Louise says, her eyes fixing on his. Her long brown hair spills down her back and arms before finishing in a pile on the bed around her voluptuous arse.

The African twists slightly around to face me before turning back to her and it occurs to me that Kojo, this champion bodybuilder, is actually nervous himself. This is the same effect Louise has on movie producers, big-shot actors and billionaire bankers alike."Hello..." his eyes are drawn to the flawless pale flesh visible between my wife's breasts, as intended.

"Call me Louise." Damn, but she sounds so fucking seductive and she's barely even trying.

He nods as I try to decide if I heard an involuntary gulp of air coming from Kojo's extensive chest, though there's no mistaking the tiny beads of sweat beginning to prick at the back of his substantial neck.

I'm already so fascinated that I'm slow to take an initial lead here. "Let me put some music on," I declare, clapping my hands, "can I get you a drink? Wine for you, Louise, Kojo, what would you like?" The truth is that a part of me just wants to evaporate into the corner to watch these two get it on naturally, but I'm here, there's no getting around it, and I'm also the common denominator, so I recognize it's on me to get things started.

"I will have a beer, Monty."

My hands are literally shaking as I rifle through the minibar, pour out a glass of red and pop the caps off two bottles. When I hand Kojo his drink I'm keen for my wife to again see us standing beside each other, close, for comparisons sake. I'm also getting off on this myself, I cannot deny it, being an inferior man physically, and my cock is already throbbing from behind my CKs. Oh, I'll have to bring myself off eventually, somehow, there's no doubt about that, though I haven't thought anywhere near that far ahead yet.

"The music!" I remember, and stride across to where there's a ready Motown playlist on my phone and then Can't Help My Self by The Four Tops is playing softly out the speakers. When I turn back Kojo and my wife are still silently appraising each other. He swallows and his Adam's apple pulses. Why aren't they getting on with it? Is it because I'm standing around like a spare part? To say I feel … not *awkward* … but certainly like a fish out of water is an understatement. It's not like we've ever done this before and after tonight, if I were to be honest, we're unlikely to ever do this again.

"Would you like me to leave?" I ask Kojo, holding my breath.

"No, I don't mind," Kojo's quick to respond. Thank God.

"Great, um, can I get you a drink?" I've already asked him that and my fists clench in embarrassment. "Sorry, I'll…" I back away a step.

"Monty," my wife's hand is touching her neck and never

did she look so fragile, feminine and perfect, "it's not too late to…"

"No!" I'm very quick to intervene. "I want to do this. How about you? You don't want to…"

"No!" She cuts me off before I get chance to finish, we're all still good, and neither does it escape my attention that she's rubbing her forearm as she flashes Kojo what I can only call an insecure glance that I don't think is an act. Perhaps she wants to do this a little more than I'd originally assumed and is worried that I might still pull the plug.

"Relax, Monty, my friend," Kojo removes his jacket, neatly folds it and places it over the back of a chair, "we are just three friends here, celebrating a beautiful wedding and getting to know each other a little better."

"Yes, I'll remember that," I run a hand through my hair and gesture for him to clink bottles, "cheers." I notice again the way my wife slowly exhales through her mouth. Relief.

"Cheers." The angle of his elbow as he holds his beer is making his biceps stretch the white sleeve of his shirt almost to the point of tearing. They make an abundance of clothes for the multitude of fat people but it must be terribly hard finding something to fit when you're built like Conan the Barbarian.

Louise is staring at Kojo's body also, her fingertips now lightly grazing back and forth across her lips. She pats the bed beside her whilst looking up at him. "Perhaps you might regale me about the time you saved my husband's life?"

Kojo emits a small laugh and loosens his tie before perching beside my wife on the edge of the bed, their rumps coming flush together, and the contrast in size is staggering, of masculine and feminine, black and white. He flashes a grin up at me. "He just swam out a little too far, that is all, but I was glad to be on hand."

"He's too modest, Louise, if it hadn't been for Kojo then you might have been met by Horace or Barnaby that day at the dealership." Everybody laughs at my remark, easing the tension significantly.

My wife angles so that she can lean into his body, her left breast unable to remain away from his shoulder. "Well then, it seems we all have much to thank you for."

"You can say that again," I laugh and feel myself beginning to relax, although that's bound to reverse as soon as the fun really starts, "and stop being so bloody modest, Kojo, you're a hero." I take another step back towards the corner and the chair that's waiting for me there, hoping to slowly dissolve into the background as the two stars take centre stage.

"Hero?" Kojo sniggers. "You are so funny, Monty." He turns towards my wife and slips a hand inside her negligee, and I feel a jealous shiver course through my body. He could so easily grab her wonderful, naked globe if he wanted, but for now he's content to squeeze the tight, flat flesh of her abdomen. Louise has a wonderful abdomen, the lines just barely visible owing to her strict fitness regimen that's all part of the job for an actress, and of course it sits just above expansive hips that bestow upon her a most wonderful hourglass figure, she's part Mediterranean, after all, though how Kojo is managing to contain himself, I have no idea.

Louise breaths heavier, closes her eyes and leans back, silently inviting the African to persist, which he does by moving his lips to her neck. Slowly, he works his way up from her delicate collar bone to the sensitive flesh just below her ear and at least twice my wife shivers uncontrollably.

He moves across her jaw, arriving at her lips from when she wastes no time throwing her arms around his neck and deepening the kiss as the sweet sigh of her breath augments against his face. It's already so hot that I dare not so much as even touch myself lest my cock explode and I'm forced to bring an immediate end to this madness. And then his hand, finally, slides up her body to envelop a large, round, perky breast, her nipple, in anticipation of him, already engorged with blood. A cry is emitted from her as she pushes her chest up harder against his hand.

He brushes the negligee from her shoulder, and then the other side, before pulling away so that he can appreciate my wife's gifts. I hear the agonized grunt from the other side of the room, as well as see the sultry, confident smile from my wife, after all, she knows what she has, what her body does to men.

Kojo growls, "fuck!" before hastily tugging the tie out from his collar and beginning work on his shirt buttons. She heaves against his shoulder, the negligee free from her breasts but now bunched around her thighs, as he continues to fumble with the buttons and two thuds signal the discarding of his shoes. When his shirt parts in the middle my wife is quick to begin tugging at his sleeves and once the garment is discarded her eyebrows rise in appreciation of his sculpted body, her lips puckering briefly before they find their way back to Kojo's.

His black hands feast on my wife, devouring her breasts as I have to fight myself to stay away from my quivering prick. My heart is pounding and my head thumping as I'm assailed by a terrible envious rage that seethes throughout me.

And I absolutely fucking love it.

There's something I have to do, urgently, while my head is in this state, and so I wait for Kojo to position his body atop my wife, to lose themselves in passionate kisses, before silently edging for the bathroom and rifling through my wife's toiletry bag. I find a single white pill encased in its foil packet and thrust it into my pocket before quietly returning to my seat and taking a much needed pull of beer.

Kojo rolls onto his side and they both start attacking his belt, yanking it out the loops and moving for the zip. I lean forwards, holding my breath, my wife now completely naked having already removed her negligee, and then Kojo's on his back working the trousers from his thighs. My wife's hand wastes no time and is already delving beneath the elastic of his white and perfectly contrasting boxers to wrap around his cock and I'm able to pull my gaze away from the incredibly prominent tent threatening to snap the elastic for long enough to catch my wife's hungry expression.

"Bloody hell, it's like my entire bloody forearm." It's a rare day when Louise curses and yet the size of Kojo's manhood has managed to achieve it.

Meanwhile, he's given up trying to tug the restrictive material of his trousers from his bulging calves dangling off the edge of the bed, my wife milking his length whilst her uncovered snatch hangs a couple of feet above his nose giving him something else to think about. Quietly, I step across towards the bed and tug the trousers from his legs, leaving only his socks, neatly folding them and placing the garment over his jacket on the chair. I then stand side-on to the action, briefly considering if I should assist with Kojo's underwear but decide against it. Fuck, but I'm so impatient. Louise, remembering I'm in the room, glances up and catches my own little tent poking through my trousers, she then glances back down to where she's heavily preoccupied, making a face that tells me there's no fucking comparison, and leans further in towards Kojo's cock as she increases the length of her strokes.

Kojo pulls her pussy down onto his face, causing her to temporarily cease what she's doing as her back arches and a delighted squeal escapes her.

"Fuck...!" I can only mumble to myself, a black man's tongue delving inside my wife's cunt. Another wave of jealous fury assaults me and I'm caught in two minds about whether or not to back away to my seat or sit on the edge of the bed for a closer view. I decide to back away, biting my bottom lip so hard that I taste blood.

Louise's eyes glaze over and I know what's happening,

she's climaxing from Kojo's tongue. She's always so very good at coming orally, which is why I'm always so keen to pleasure her this way, as vaginal orgasms are few and far between for her, despite how hard I try bringing her off that way too. Her body phases between moments of tense rigidity and flaccidness as she wrings out her orgasm and only when she recovers does she eagerly shove Kojo's boxers down his thighs.

His size catches on the elastic and bends back to a point beyond the vertical that almost looks uncomfortable but Louise angles him to the side and pulls the elastic over the top of his swollen bulb, the sudden release of tension causing his entire length to recoil back against his abdomen with an audible slap, leaving a small quantity of pre-cum on the top two muscles of his six pack.

Holy fuck!

I subconsciously back away, gaping at him, my wife's *"entire fucking forearm"* is no exaggeration. Not at all. I mean, I'd seen him three years ago in Ghana, but only in the soft, and at the time I'd doubted he could even grow much more than that. Turns out he can. And does! And Belle had taken all this monster? Maybe that's the reason she's been unable to hold down a steady relationship ever since? Because after Kojo she's unable to feel any other man inside of her? Or maybe she's been stretched out so wide that neither can any man discern any pleasure from the act himself. The possibility is alarming. What *will* sex with my wife feel like after she's taken this python? Will she be forever changed for the worse? The chance of such a happening almost forces me to bring an end to this madness immediately and yet, conversely, it's the very thing that more than anything else makes me want to persist.

Louise has to open wide to get her lips around him and even then she's just barely swallowing his big, fat, round, shiny, dark head. Kojo groans and thrusts up with his hips but this only forces my wife's head back. Instead, she gives him more stimulation by using her hand to once again commence with long strokes from the base working all the way up his shaft as a thick vein works hard keeping him flush with blood. I edge towards the bed and move down to my knees for a closer look, and can't help but fix on my wife's moist, red lips as they clasp around that dark mushroom while from not far away a series of smacks and slurps rebound from my wife's cunt, her hips thrusting in and out of Kojo's face, his fingers sinking hard into her buttocks. Sweet little hums emanate from my wife and I don't even think she's aware she's doing it.

Again, I fix on Kojo's stunning length and the gap his girth forces between my wife's thumb and fingers as she vainly attempts to wrap her entire hand around his width. Briefly, I consider adding a hand myself, just for a few strokes, to know how it feels, after all, there's room for two, but I decide against it. No, because doing such a thing would only pull myself, not to mention my wife, out of the moment, and there's no telling how the bull might react to being jerked off by me.

Just step back and enjoy it, Monty.

Louise pulls away as Kojo draws another climax from my wife. She's mushing her crotch hard against his face now, shivering as her eyes roll back in her head. It feels strange watching from close by as my wife is pleasured by another man and only now, for the first time, do I realize my entire body is shaking too. I fix on the colour contrast between them, which could hardly clash more, and it's the hottest thing in the whole fucking world.

Louise rolls off Kojo and he's quick to manhandle her around before their lips press passionately again together. He throws her knee over his considerable body so that she's straddling him, his back propped up by two pillows. She leans forwards, crushing her breasts against his chest whilst reaching back to again seize his organ. Considering the fact he's uncovered, I'm not sure if she intends to steer him towards her opening. It's not something we've discussed, ensuring Kojo wore a rubber whilst fucking my wife, though thinking about it now the fact the morning after pill *was* mentioned implies it's probably not necessary. Besides, I want nothing more than just about anything else in the world than to watch this African stud nut inside my wife, uncovered. Regardless, Kojo's raging length is reaching a good way up her back and she's nowhere near high up enough on her knees to guide him inside, and right now he's holding her hips down against his abdomen with a bodybuilder's grip. No, he's definitely seasoned, alright, and can control his urges despite the quality of woman he's about to enter, and I'm thinking that right now he'd like to enjoy himself some more first.

He does so by digitally stimulating her beautiful engorged pearl before moving onto her folds and slowly inserting a finger. Louise hitches back with a sharp exhalation, the same reaction that's so familiar to me because she does this every time I enter her with my dick. He delves further inside and after a bit of mushing about retracts his finger so that he can enter with a second. This is an act I'm always careful about not engaging in myself, in fact, I'm quite paranoid about not doing it because down there I only just compare favourably to two fingers. Looking at Kojo, however, I'm getting the impression he definitely doesn't suffer from that same paranoia.

Finally, unable to take it anymore, Kojo wraps his arms around Louise's waist and lifts her off the bed, plonking her down so that the broad expanse of her Mediterranean hips, along with her dripping wet pussy, are presented and waiting for his enormous length. In the meantime, I've somehow found myself back in my seat, leaning forward covered in sweat. Now, Kojo leans over my wife's back to grasp her hanging breasts as he whispers something in her ear, something just for her, words I'll never get to know. She nods and Kojo straightens, one hand on her tiny waist, the other halfway down his shaft so that he can angle the tip and part her flaps. *He's not asking permission to go in bare either*, is all I can think, a second before he's pushing between her lips.

"Aaaawweeee..." my wife never does that when I enter her.

But more to the point ... there's a huge, dark African man entering my wife!

I collapse back in my seat but then lean immediately forward again. Sweat pours down my face and back as I'm overcome by a terrible, and yet delicious, seething frustration. Never before in my life has my cock throbbed so painfully and keeping my hand from touching it is the hardest thing I've ever had to do.

Kojo continues sinking slowly inside, inch after dark, meaty inch, pausing halfway to allow the tight constraints of Louise's pussy time to adjust. He maintains a strong grip on her waist but slides down to her arse when he again starts squeezing forwards. "Fuck, you are tight..." it's an insult to my own manhood, no doubt about it, even if it wasn't intended that way, and my fists answer by clenching hard around the armrests. Finally, he bottoms out, tugging Louise's buttocks firmly into his crotch whilst no doubt his size is forcing her cervix against her womb.

"Aaawweeeeeeeeee...! I thought you were never going to stop," she just manages to hiss. She arches her back in that devastatingly sexy way she does to give the man looking down from above, usually me, the best possible view of her considerable curves.

"Fuck! You are so sexy..." Kojo groans as he pulls her buttocks so hard into his hips that the veins in his biceps pop and protrude menacingly. "I hate to see you go but I love to watch you leave." He slowly, ever so carefully, pulls out, and I envision the gaping chasm left behind where his thickness has perhaps forever widened her, but this is quickly refilled when he again pushes forwards.

Louise makes a sound I can't even hope to describe and then she's flexing her hips, using her tight cunt to milk Kojo's manhood even as he remains balls deep inside of her. She likes to do this with me, indeed, I love it when she does this too, as being in control of the movement in attempts to hit all her right spots is the closest she's able to come to achieving a vaginal orgasm, at least with me. Of course, it hardly helps when I can only reach about five and a half inches deep and I so often blow my load within minutes of starting, but by doing this we've come pretty close on a number of occasions.

"Haaaaaaaaaa…" she starts.

What the fuck?

"That is right, Louise," hearing him say my wife's name, for whatever reason, brings this, what we're doing, all the more home, "come on, you can do it."

"Aaaaaaaaaahhhhhh…"

"That is right, enjoy it, enjoy it, beautiful lady." He tilts back with his mouth wide open because I'm guessing that right now my wife's cunt is gripping him like a fucking vice.

My eyes widen. "So size really fucking does matter," I can only stutter as a feeling of inferiority swirls through me. Not once in more than two years of marriage have I managed to make Louise come with my dick and yet Kojo's managed it within a matter of seconds.

"Oh … my … fucking … god!" Louise twists around to face him as best she's able, her eyes animalistic and wild.

Kojo reaches under her to give her breasts another appreciative squeeze. "That should make it easier for me to move now." He commences in earnest with his thrusts, pulling slowly out before pushing delightfully back inside, repeating, over and over, again and again, slowly so that he can feel and experience my wife's tightness, gradually building in speed so that he can better slake his carnal urges, occasionally changing angles and hitting new spots that prompts a different unearthly sound from my wife. When he starts pounding her arse like a starving man does a fillet of prime steak with a tenderizing mallet, my fingers are digging so hard into the armrests that I split the leather. I swear, but if I don't see to my own needs, and soon, then I'll be firing inside my underwear and creating the biggest mess this side of Lagos.

I stand in readiness for the finale and find my feet are taking me of their own volition closer to the action. I fix on Kojo's soot-black meat buried deep between my wife's pink lips surrounded by the most beautiful of white flesh, the red impressions in her tiny waist where his fingertips have been digging in, and finally the even larger red marks on her buttocks caused by the power of his thrusts.

By now my wife is screaming, a constant string of curses, blasphemes and his name. "Kojo, Kojo, oh Jesus … fucking … Christ … yes … Kojo!"

Finally, he grits his teeth and all the muscles in his body tense as he prepares to release his seed. For a moment, I wonder if he's about to pull out, to fire over her buttocks and back, but no, he doesn't pull out, and truth is I never really expected him to, nor wanted it. No, men like this take what they want. "Uuughhhhhh…" and then he's fully rooted, all the way to his balls, as his entire body bucks and convulses, and stream after hot, sticky stream of thick nigger cum is firing against my wife's womb even as her body, deep in the throes of its own climax, works to squeeze every last drop out from him, to suck his cream as close as possible towards the precious egg that's ready and waiting to be fertilized.

They both flop to the bed, what's almost certainly a thirteen-inch cock still fully hilted.

There's only silence announcing the awkward part following a life-changing event that's now over. My wife's arm dangles off the edge of the bed. I take her hand and kiss her knuckles. "Enjoy the rest of your night, my dear." She doesn't even acknowledge me.

With the sweet, musty stench of sex filling the room, I slowly exit and quietly close the door behind me. Outside, the corridor's empty. Good. There's a chance that an untold amount of humiliation might be coming my way, but until that day arrives, *if* it arrives, then my wife's honour must be safeguarded.

I have the key for the room I reserved for Kojo. Down the corridor. I enter. Empty. Not even his bags. I'm so fucking horny, so hot and fucking bothered, so riled that if I wait to act until later, when my nut's spilled and I'm thinking straight again then I'll never go through with it, with this next important part.

I rush for the bathroom, fumble Louise's morning after pill from my pocket, pop it from the packet and flush it down the toilet. "Fuck...!" But it's done. It's really fucking done!

Shaking uncontrollably, I collapse to the bed, my trousers and underwear already bunched around my ankles and commence wanking my five-and-a-half-inch freckly prick. It's not even ten seconds before I'm jizzing three feet into the air, covering my legs, pubes, wrist, hand and sheets with my worthless spunk.

The single, greatest, most powerful orgasm of my entire life.

I don't sleep. All throughout the night, I'm restless. Twice more I wank myself off, the second time after creeping into the corridor at four in the morning and spending a few minutes listening to my wife still hollering and howling from behind our bedroom door. It drives me crazy.

Now, at a little after nine, some of the wedding guests will be leaving their rooms and going down for breakfast. I shower, change into clean clothes and cautiously head back to our suite, opening the door and entering. I step inside, my heart beating insanely and find the bed empty.

My heart shoots into my mouth.

Surely they wouldn't head down together for breakfast?

Then, finally, the gentle patters of water penetrate the bathroom door and I realize they're taking a shower as feminine giggles are punctuated by the occasional higher-pitched sigh or masculine grunt.

I settle into the chair and try to relax, hard as it is. The room reeks of sweat and sex, the bed is a mess and there are spatters of what can only be blood on the sheets.

My head's clearer now, marginally, and I can't help but fixate on the precious morning after pill that last night, in my monstrously agitated and horny state, I'd flushed down the fucking toilet. It had been worth it, at least at the time, but now I'm very conscious to the potential consequences of my actions.

The bathroom door opens and Kojo exits with a towel wrapped around his midsection. "Monty, my friend," he says as though we're meeting for a fucking drink at the bar. My wife follows close behind wearing only a loose gown. Her hair's wet and reaches all the way down to her barely covered hips. When she sees me she immediately frowns and breaks eye contact. Oh, I get it, she wanted one final round before saying goodbye to her black lover.

"Hi, darling," I kiss her on the cheek, "how are you this morning?"

"I'm good," she says simply, unable to hide the disappointment in her tone.

"Monty," Kojo snatches up his shirt, "I will get dressed and leave you both to enjoy your day."

I nod and the next five minutes are tense whilst he dresses. I spend the time pretending to be engrossed in my phone.

When he's done I show him to the door and hold out my hand. "Thank you, Kojo, for last night. Enjoy the rest of your stay."

He takes my hand but I can't help but feel a little disturbed by the subtle way the side of his mouth curls up, like there's something I've missed. "I will." He glances beyond me to Louise and a sick feeling further manifests in my stomach. Why isn't she rushing over to say goodbye to him? Shouldn't she be?

I look from Louise back to Kojo. "Um, how long are you in the country for anyway?" It only occurs to me now that this is a question I haven't thought to ask.

The African glances at my wife and then back to me. "I haven't decided yet."

"Huh," it comes out of me as an anxious breath, "well, goodbye, Kojo," I say with a deliberate finality.

Finally, my wife steps over and kisses him on the cheek. "Goodbye, Kojo." It seems paltry considering everything. Perhaps if they hadn't been getting along so well then a peck on the cheek might have been understandable but from the state of the bed they've been fucking all throughout the night, indeed, they've just taken a shower together.

"Goodbye." There's that smirk again, and then Kojo's glancing to his left, right, and stepping away.

I shut the door after him and spend a moment with my hand still on the handle. I twist around. Louise has already turned away and is now in the bathroom. From the sound of the rustling, I assume she's searching through her bag. The pill! Looks like we're about to have *that* conversation. I open the window and take a breath in preparation.

After a minute she steps out and gives me a sideward glance. "Monty?"

"Yes?" I brace myself.

"So, what are we doing for breakfast?"

Most of the guests, including myself, have filthy hangovers. Kojo's gone, which is a relief, and a different kind of party rages today, all day, one that's more relaxed; coffees, brunches, dinners, even a friendly game of polo on the lawn. Additionally, there are so many old friends still present that I'm finding it impossible to drag Louise away, only a morning after pill on my mind. Besides, it's Sunday, we're in the countryside and the only open pharmacies will likely be miles away back in London, which is another problem because we were originally intending to spend a second night here at Carrington Hall. We'll almost certainly be safe with Louise taking an emergency contraceptive tomorrow, though how I'll get her to take it without her knowing I flushed the other is another thing entirely. More perplexing still is why, come late Sunday, she still hasn't brought up the subject, I mean, considering the urgency of the situation, isn't she curious about why I've not broached the subject either, maybe stood by and watched as she swallowed it? Becoming increasingly concerned, as I catch her discretely sending what has to be the tenth text message apparently to her sister, Karla, I deign to slip one in her porridge tomorrow morning, which means leaving for London right fucking now and stopping at the first dispensary we pass.

On the motorway, my foot hits the floor of my Lamborghini Sesto Elemento as we speed towards the capital, and an open pharmacy, with a rare urgency. I've been faking a cough these last couple of hours so an excuse has already been planted.

"Darling," she begins, her hand reaching over to touch my knee, "I'll be up early tomorrow morning, Karla needs me to help decorate her new flat."

"You what?" I say more abruptly than intended.

"And it's possible she might need me to stay the night, you know, just in case we don't finish the hallway."

My grip around the wheel tightens as I feel my imperative plans going to shit, and quite possibly the rest of my life. "You can't!"

"What? And why not?" She gives me an angry glare and my objection wilts away.

"Nothing." After a short silence, I follow up with, "um, so that's who you've been texting all day, is it?"

She blinks and her sweet demeanour returns. "Of course."

I chew on my lip. "I thought Karla was moving next month?"

"She was," she says, naturally, "but she found a place she really liked and had to close the deal quickly."

"Oh." I shrug. "Where?"

"Hmm, Whitechapel."

<hr>

I'M LEFT with no options. I must supplant Kojo's seed with my own, by any means necessary, or else be left carrying a baby that's not mine, and a fucking black one at that.

Come bedtime, it's time to fuck like my lineage depends on it.

I'm quick with the foreplay and manage to get myself extra hard by thinking about Kojo impregnating my wife. Yes, I'm aware of the sick irony here, but if this is the best imagery to make me hard then I'm more than willing to run with it. I lie atop Louise, our lips locked in passion. She reaches down and steers me inside. My eyebrows furrow in confusion. Something doesn't feel right.

"Am I in?" I ask, the panic evident in my tone.

Louise squints. "Um, I'm not sure, honey."

I throw off the covers, place my weight on my elbows and glance between our bodies. "I *am* fucking in."

We share a look that words cannot even hope to describe, though it's obvious we both know what the issue is. Bizarrely, despite the seriousness of the situation, my boner's harder than ever and so I plough on despite the fact I can't feel a fucking thing, after all, by this point what else is there I can even fucking do? From the look on her face, Louise can't feel very much, if anything, either, but she squeezes her cunt as hard as she can, and for as long as she's able without giving herself cramp, but on three separate occasions I slip out of her, once without even realizing it.

After thirty minutes, by which time usually I could finish several times, we give up and instead Louise uses her mouth to suck my seed out from my dick. Quickly, she jumps from the bed and all I can do is stare on forlornly as she spits my firstborn child down the toilet and flushes it away.

From the Author

Thanks for reading.

At this point I have no plans for any marketing material, Facebook fan pages or email newsletters. If you like my work and would like to be informed of any future releases then the best thing to do might be to subscribe to me via the 'Follow the Author' button on the Amazon sales page for this book.

If you've enjoyed this book then please feel free to write a few words in the form of a review on the page where you made the purchase.

Meanwhile, please check out my other books…

War Booty
My Dark Secret
War Restitution
A Plantation Scandal

Thanks so much.

Aspen Berry

AVAILABLE NOW ON AMAZON!

AVAILABLE NOW ON AMAZON!

WITH WAR COMES SPOILS
WAR
Booty
ASPEN BERRY